A Bleeding Hearts Valley Thriller

FAMILY TREE

SARA LEA

FAMILY TREE

A BLEEDING HEARTS VALLEY THRILLER

SARA LEA

Porkchop Publishing LLC
2709 N Hayden Island Drive STE 417603
Portland, OR 97217

COVER DESIGN BY: M.A. GREEN

A BLEEDING HEARTS VALLEY THRILLER

Welcome to Bleeding Hearts Valley, a standalone series of interconnected thrillers in one twisted midwestern suburb.

Keep coming back to *Bleeding Hearts Valley* to uncover more dark secrets. But before moving in, remember, you can never trust your neighbors.

Unhinged by Danielle Fear
I Saw You Sweetheart by Erica Damon
An Abrupt Departure by P.D. Workman
Family Tree by Sara Lea

PROLOGUE

THE RAIN HAS BEEN SO *heavy today. I'm glad we are tucked in, safe and cozy. No place to go. Just a night at home, working on my crafts.*

From my kitchen window, I can see the rain pouring in their backyard—the ground soggy and wet. Lots of mud. She came outside while I was watching, pacing around, inspecting the grass. I had no idea what she was doing so late at night outside in the rain. She circled her lawn like a dog looking for a place to go potty.

Then she started digging.

Frantic. With a feverish strength I didn't know she had.

I'm worried about her, but there's only so much I can do. Who knew what she's gotten herself into, but I have a feeling now is not the time to go check on her.

I watch for a few minutes and then go back to my crochet project. I can always check on her tomorrow.

I must have dozed off in the middle of my project, because I'm jolted awake to the sound of an engine starting.

Getting up, I look out the window. His truck is backing out of the driveway, but I'm pretty sure that's not him in the driver's seat. The winter cap pulled down low isn't fooling me. She's driving off in his vehicle.

I might seem like the pushy, nosy old lady next door, but I'm not. I just like to be neighborly.

I want to be a good neighbor.

And what I'm going to do tonight is; be a good neighbor the best way I know how.

I'm going to mind my own business.

CHAPTER ONE

I STARED AT MY CELLPHONE. I didn't need a reminder of the missed call. Yet there it was, still sitting in my notification banner. I swiped to clear it. I had listened to the voicemail three times already and could probably recite it back verbatim, but I wasn't ready to call the number back.

Although the woman who left the message was vague when requesting I call her back urgently, I was procrastinating because there was only one reason I'd get a call from Valleyview South Hospital—the small hospital in my hometown.

Mom.

Just thinking that word was like a punch to the gut. I hadn't really had a mom in years. Not the way I should have. The mom I had grown up with had deserted me.

I actually hadn't spoken to anyone at all from Bleeding Hearts Valley in over ten years, not even my own mother. Maybe she was in the hospital, unable to call me herself. Or worse.

I wasn't ready to face the possibility of *or worse* just yet. That would close the door to ever reconciling.

Right now, I could believe my mother was still alive. Maybe she was sick. She would recover. *Maybe she had surgery and needs help*, I told myself. Of course, my mother would have been able to call herself if that was the case. Deep down, I knew these explanations didn't make sense.

I did not know what my mother's health had been like. Mom had told me never to come back to Bleeding Hearts Valley, and I had tried to reach out at first, but eventually couldn't take the rejection anymore. *What happens when your own mother suddenly turns on you?*

Well, what happened to me was that I closed down that chapter in my life. Closed down the possibility of reconciling so I didn't have to go through the pain of that loss again.

I had made the trek back to college years ago, leaving Bleeding Hearts Valley behind, after the Thanksgiving break when my father died. When Mom told me not to come back, it broke my heart. I'd vowed not to think about my hometown again, and to move forward, forget the past. And that'd worked out so far.

So what if I was too damaged to form any genuine connection with anyone in the city? I had a fantastic job reviewing contracts for a big-name law firm, enjoyed happy hours with colleagues, and occasionally went out on a date. I didn't have a best friend and hadn't had one since I'd stopped talking to Vanessa that Thanksgiving break. I hadn't gone beyond the first couple of dates with anyone, but I had a good life. I was happy. Mostly. The heartache of not having parents or family—especially a mother—even I couldn't deny it had changed me forever.

Willing the nerves in my stomach to settle, I brushed

my hair out of my face and slowly lowered my thumb to the button to call the number back. Lifting the phone to my ear, I exhaled slowly and squeezed my eyes shut, as if that would ease the blow. Whatever was coming, I wasn't prepared.

The woman that answered the phone sounded annoyed—until I announced who I was and that I was returning a call. The immediate change in the woman's tone made my stomach drop. My ears rang, and I tried to focus on what she was saying. The smell of lilacs—my mother's scent—enveloped me, and the room swayed and darkened.

"Are you still there, Ms. Jenkins? Did you hear me?" The woman interrupted my thoughts.

"I... yes. Yes, I'm here," I answered numbly. The room spun, and I blinked rapidly, trying to steady myself.

"I'm so sorry for your loss, but we need to know..." The phone slipped from my grasp as it clattered to the floor and the room went black.

When I came to, I fanned my face, heat coursing through my veins. Pulling myself over to the couch, I leaned back against it so I could collect myself. Standing up wasn't an option—I didn't trust that I could stay upright.

It wasn't the *first* time I had blacked out, although it had been such a long time since it happened. I shuddered to think, my world was falling apart again. I'd spent so long—so many years—trying to keep myself from feeling anything that deeply.

I blinked away tears, refusing to cry. Refusing to let

those emotions sweep me away. *Don't cry. Don't think. Don't feel.*

But my emotions took over, and I reflected back on the last time I remembered blacking out. The phone call from Mom that destroyed me.

"Grace, you can't come home for Christmas. I've paid the extra fee for you to stay in the dorms over break. It's best if you stay there. You can't come home again," Mom had said.

"But what will I do for Christmas?" I asked. Mom had mumbled about having already mailed me gifts.

But what I had been thinking about was the meal that I always helped Mom and Aunt Clara put together. After we had stuffed ourselves on the feast, we would sit around the table putting together a puzzle.

I hadn't even absorbed that Mom had said I couldn't come home again. That realization wouldn't come until much later—when I was told I wasn't coming home for the summer either.

On this call, Mom had cut me off and ended the call abruptly, refusing to answer any of my questions. The smell of lilacs overwhelmed me—and then I blacked out.

Pulling myself back to the present, I picked up my phone and called the number back again. I knew the woman was waiting for my call—no doubt waiting to find out what to do with the body.

The body.

I still couldn't believe it. Mom was dead. It was surreal. We hadn't talked for so long, and now we never would.

No chance to repair things. No chance of having my mother back in my life. Ever. It was so final.

The woman picked up right away, clearly expecting my return call. I apologized, and she murmured comforting words. It was obvious she did this a lot—she knew all the right things to say.

But really… None of this was right.

"I hate to bring this up, I know you might need time to decide, but we *will* need to know where we should have the body sent." As gently as she said it, the word *body* broke something in me, cracking my chest wide open.

"Send her to Browns' Funeral Home." My face felt numb as I answered. I couldn't remember where I'd heard that name. And I didn't know if they even did cremations. Or were still open. But my mouth seemed to move despite my mind reeling.

"Okay, we can do that. Again, I'm so sorry for your loss." Her voice had a lilt of pity to it. Practiced or genuine, it didn't matter. It made me feel worse.

"Wait, I… you didn't say… what- what happened to her? I mean, how…" My voice trailed off as I stumbled over the words. There was a long pause and I started to wonder if she'd already hung up.

"She had a heart attack. A neighbor found her in her back garden," the woman answered gently.

I covered my mouth and choked back the sob that was creeping up my throat. I blurted out a goodbye and ended the call. Knowing she had died alone outside like that, so suddenly—it made it all feel worse.

The heaviness that came over me—realizing I had to go home and take care of everything—was a weight I wasn't sure I could bear. I wondered why it hadn't been Aunt Clara who had called. Surely Mom would have at least reached out if anything had happened to my aunt, wouldn't she?

Would she have? A sudden burst of anger rocked my core. It wasn't fair that I had to go home and deal with this. Mom had told me not to come back—I didn't know why. Although I had begged and pleaded for an answer, Mom had sent me a letter instead, refusing to discuss it with me. When I next tried to call her, a robotic voice let me know the number was disconnected. My calls to Aunt Clara had gone unanswered.

And now here I was, blacking out again, taking me back to those lonely, vulnerable years I thought I'd left behind. It had been a frequent occurrence at one point—the buildup of drama or distress, and I would black out. But around the end of my college years, I got myself together enough. I had focused on living the most mundane, boring life, not letting anyone else in for so long, so I could avoid any emotional shocks.

Life had felt safe. It *had* been safe. But now, with one brief phone call, it was all ripped away.

BLEEDING HEARTS VALLEY
BEHAVIORAL HEALTH SERVICES SOUTH

Client Name: Grace Jenkins
Age: 16
Date of Intake: 10/4/2008
Referred By: Mark Anderson, MD
Present at Intake: Grace and mother, Heidi Jenkins
Demographics:
Grace is a 16-year-old female residing at home with both parents. Father was reported to be at work and was unable to attend the intake session.
Presenting Concerns:
Grace was referred by her pediatrician for evaluation due to recurrent episodes of loss of consciousness or fainting in response to stressful or fear-inducing situations. According to mother's report, these "spells" have occurred over several years with increasing frequency. During these episodes, Grace reportedly loses awareness and later has no recollection of events, recalling only the experience of "coming to."
Relevant Medical Information:
Pediatric evaluation has ruled out medical or neurological causes for these episodes. Pediatrician suspects a psychogenic or stress-related component and recommended psychological assessment and therapy.
Observations:
Both Grace and her mother presented as cooperative but guarded throughout the intake. They provided limited detail regarding the episodes, attributing them primarily to test anxiety and academic stress. Affect appeared constricted, and Grace maintained minimal eye contact, responding briefly to direct questions.
Plan of Care/ Recommendations:
Further assessment is indicated to explore the psychological and environmental factors contributing to Grace's episodes. Ongoing individual therapy is recommended to address anxiety, coping skills, and stress response.

Intake Practitioner: Peter Aderman, LMSW

CHAPTER TWO

I THOUGHT sleep would never come that night, and when it did, it was light—waking every hour on the hour, sheet tangled around my legs like I had been wrestling with it, t-shirt damp with sweat and clinging to my chest. Morning came, my eyes swollen and red, crease lines on my cheek.

I crawled out of my bed, the thick comforter falling to the floor. I padded into the kitchen, welcoming the cool feel of tile on my bare feet.

While the coffee was brewing, I gulped down a glass of ice water, leaning into the fridge until I shivered from being in a now-cold, sweaty shirt.

Planting myself at the kitchen table, I tucked my legs up on the chair in front of me, resting my chin on my knees as I watched the coffee drip into my cup. It was hypnotic and soothing in a way. I tried to make my mind focus, but my thoughts raced from one thing to the next.

With a hot cup of black coffee cupped in my palm, I moved from the kitchen to the living room. I was crawling out of the brain fog. Curling up on the couch, I sipped the scalding coffee, feeling my tastebuds painfully protest.

I would have to go home and help take care of things. I didn't know why Aunt Clara hadn't called me, and I wasn't even sure where to start. We didn't have any other family.

I dialed her old number—one of the few numbers I knew by heart. I hadn't tried it in years—and when I had, she hadn't answered, but the number was etched in my memory like everything else that haunted me. *This number has been disconnected,* the automated message informed me, but it took me a minute to compute this. Did Aunt Clara change her number?

I was about to get online and start searching when my phone rang. Nearly dropping it, I stared at the screen. I didn't recognize the number, but it was the Bleeding Hearts Valley area code, so I hit ANSWER.

"Ms. Jenkins?" The man at the other end of the line paused for my confirmation. When I responded, he continued. "I'm sorry about your mother's… passing. My name is James Addison—I'm the attorney handling her estate. She left everything in pretty good order—and I'm calling to go over a few things with you."

"Oh… I… I just found out last night. I assumed my Aunt Clara would have been handling things," I stuttered, taken aback by how quickly things were moving.

"Well, that's one thing I needed to discuss. I'm aware you weren't in contact with your family." He paused, the judgment dripping from his voice. I guessed my mother told him that much but didn't bother explaining it was her choice, not mine. He cleared his throat before continuing. "Your aunt—she isn't… well." I could tell he deliberated over the phrase to use, which puzzled me.

"She's sick?" I blurted out.

"No, not sick exactly. Mentally unwell. For a few years now. She's being cared for in a nursing home because of mental deterioration. So there is also a power of attorney to transfer over—and of course your mother's assets to discuss. This would all be best to discuss in person. Are you planning to be here soon?"

The question threw me for a loop. Of course, I'd have to go back to Bleeding Hearts Valley… I knew it, yet I'd denied it to myself all night.

I scheduled an appointment to meet with the attorney the following week; everything about this felt surreal. After hanging up, I sat and stared at the wall for what seemed like five minutes, but a quick glance at the clock told me it had been almost an hour. I'd lost a block of time staring at a blemish in the paint on the wall… I had to pull myself together.

I looked up the nursing home the attorney had given me the name of and called them. I wasn't sure what to say —I didn't know how bad Aunt Clara was. *Would they let me talk to her? Could she even talk to me?*

I wasn't surprised that they wouldn't tell me much about Aunt Clara—but I was shocked when they told me she hadn't been notified about my mother's death. Hesitantly, the woman on the phone made a vague reference to the fact that Aunt Clara wouldn't understand anyway, and it would cause unnecessary distress. She seemed to want to say more, the hesitation in her voice obvious.

I had let her know I would contact them again soon, once I had the power of attorney transferred to me, and hung up the phone, feeling even more lost than before. I would see my aunt in person when I got to town. It was probably better that way, anyway. It would be difficult to assess her condition over the phone.

What happened to Aunt Clara? A new feeling of dread built in me, flooding through my body. This was so much more than my mother passing away. There was so much to uncover, so much to discover. I didn't know if I was ready.

I got a whiff of lilacs. *No, not again. Not now.* I took deep calming breaths, but it did nothing to stop the blackness that surrounded me and took over as I passed out again.

WHITE OAK MANOR

Incident Report - Clara Miller
Date/Time: 5/6/2015 8:00 PM
Location: Facility garden

At approximately 8:00PM, resident Clara Miller was observed outside the facility, unaccompanied, in the garden area. The resident was found kneeling and digging in the soil with her hands. Upon approach, resident was noted to be speaking incoherently, referencing "fixing the garden."

When staff attempted to escort resident back inside, she became agitated and combative, exhibiting physical resistance. Sedation was administered as per standing order to ensure resident and staff safety. Resident was subsequently assisted indoors, cleaned, and returned to bed without further incident.

This represents the fourth occurrence of similar behavior since admission. Episodes appear to correlate with rain or inclement weather conditions. All staff have been notified, and increased supervision and monitoring will be implemented during identified trigger conditions.

Filed by: Julie Blair, RN
Date/Time of Report: 5/6/2015 8:45PM

CHAPTER THREE

STARING DOWN AT MY SUITCASES, it occurred to me I didn't own many personal items. It had never bothered me before, but looking around my barren apartment —so sterile and institution-like, I was almost sad seeing that most of my belongings fit in those two suitcases. Clothes, toiletries, a journal, a couple of books. Everything I needed to bring with me when I left the following day.

The small couch I owned was comfortable but the blandest shade of sage green, with two small barely functional throw pillows on it. A plain wooden rectangular coffee table. And a standard flat-screen TV mounted above the fireplace. Everything in my apartment was bland. I didn't even own a bookshelf—I preferred to borrow from the library. My suitcases sat next to the front door; my briefcase containing my laptop leaned against one.

I'd used packing as an excuse to fixate on something. To not think about why I was packing. To not call my work to make official plans.The task had kept me preoccupied, and for just a moment, I'd been so focused on packing and what I needed, that I'd been able to avoid thinking about anything else.

Now it was done, and I had nothing else to do, and had to stop procrastinating the thing I needed to do next.

I clicked on CONTACTS on my phone screen and tapped my boss's name. I had been avoiding calling her. A brief text this morning had gotten me the day off—I rarely requested any—but I was going to have to tell her what happened. It was time to get it over with. I prepared myself for the pity that would ooze from her voice, making me wish the floor would swallow me whole.

I didn't talk about my personal life at work. I had never taken any time off work before for anything other than educational retreats, or the occasional virus. My boss, Andi, was the closest thing I even had to an actual friend, and she wasn't even my friend. We had a strictly professional relationship.

"Grace? I'm surprised to hear from you. I assumed you must be pretty sick or have something major going on. You never take time off." Andi answered the phone.

"Actually… I needed to talk to you about my schedule. My mother…" I paused, choking back an unexpected sob. My eyes burned with the impending tears, my response shocking me more than it probably surprised Andi. I suppressed the urge to wail and scream, fighting down the instinct to pour my heart out. "… my mother passed away. I'm going to need to go back to my hometown for a bit—I would like to work remotely full time, although I'll probably need time off to deal with… everything," I rattled off, and then gasped for a breath at the end.

"Oh, Grace, I'm so sorry to hear that. You can absolutely take off as much time as you need, and I know you love coming into the office for work, but you know our policy is that the choice is yours—you can always work remotely." Andi's soothing words only made me feel like I was tipping closer off the edge. I didn't want anyone to be sympathetic and kind. Right now I needed a distraction—I wanted to be angry instead of this aching. But I thanked her and promised to pick up anything I needed from the office before I left town and finished the call as quickly as possible.

The call left me completely drained, like a vampire had sucked me dry. I melted into my bed, intent on taking a nap after my restless night. My eyes swam with tears, and I finally let them fall, curling into a fetal position, squeezing my pillow to me as I sobbed.

I braced myself for the familiar pull—the slide into blackness that always came when the world became too much. But it didn't come. Instead, a band inside me snapped open, and the sobs tore their way out before I could stop them. They ripped through my chest, raw and violent, like they were being dragged backward through my body. Each breath felt as if it was scraping against bone.

It was ugly, humiliating, and I couldn't control it. But in the middle of it—between the gasps and the salt sting in my throat—I felt a shift. Maybe this was what release feels like. Maybe this was what I'd been holding back, the thing that had been festering and turning itself into blackouts. For the first time, I wondered if breaking apart like this wasn't a failure at all, but the only way I would stop disappearing.

HEIDI JENKINS' VOICEMAIL LOG
APRIL 2012

Voicemail from Grace Jenkins – 4/5/12 8:47 PM
"Mom? Why won't you pick up? I'm tired of leaving messages, mom. I don't understand. What did I do? I miss you. I want to come home this summer."

Voicemail from Grace Jenkins – 4/8/12 6:32 PM
"Mom, I'm starting to get worried. Are you okay? I tried to call Aunt Clara but she doesn't answer either. I'm getting scared. Mom, please call me back!"

Voicemail from Grace Jenkins – 4/11/12 3:34 PM
"(indecipherable) Please call me back mommy. I love you. I don't know what I did wrong."

Voicemail from Grace Jenkins – 4/15/12 7:12 PM
"Mom? I've left you dozens of messages. I'm getting nervous. School ends soon- I want to come home. Mom please just.. Call me back?"

Voicemail from Grace Jenkins – 4/22/12 5:23 PM
"Hi Mom. I got your letter. I don't understand why I can't call you anymore. I … I'm going to get a summer job and stay here like you said. I went to look at the apartment you leased yesterday, and it's fine… but Mom, I really miss you. I want to come home."

CHAPTER FOUR

THE DRIVE into Bleeding Hearts Valley was shorter than I remembered. Or maybe I wasn't ready to be 'home' yet. As I drove into town, all the familiar buildings looked the same but different. A sense of dread was growing in the pit of my stomach, building acid that bubbled up in my throat, threatening to choke me.

I drove around town, re-familiarizing myself with the streets to delay going home. But finally, I turned onto Monmouth Drive, my pulse throbbing in my ears. I forced myself to inhale and exhale deeply. I didn't need to black out while I was driving.

Despite my efforts to delay the inevitable, I was suddenly *home*; the house looming before me as I pulled into the driveway. Putting the car in park, I studied the front of the house.

Overgrown bushes and weeds made it look unkempt. Loose shingles flapping on the roof, paint peeling off the siding, and a broken step all screamed for attention. I couldn't believe how badly the house had fallen into shambles in the thirteen years I'd been gone.

The attorney had promised to leave a key under the doormat and to have a cleaning service stop by to take out the trash. I pulled myself out of my car, feeling weighed down, as though my pockets were filled with huge rocks. Everything in my body screamed to get back in the car, turn around, and drive back out of town.

I trudged my way up the front steps, carefully sidestepping the broken brick. The neighborhood was oddly quiet for midafternoon. Bending down, I lifted the edge of the old frayed doormat, grabbing the envelope with my name on it. I opened the flap and tipped the key into my hand. *Open the door.* I paused, conflicted. I couldn't do this. But I had no choice.

I slid the key into the doorknob, turning until it clicked. Twisting the knob, I pushed and let the front door fall open. Once I stepped inside, the first thing that hit me was the strong lemon scent of the cleaner my mother always loved. It intermingled with a fainter, musty smell—likely from the house being closed up for over a week.

Wandering through the house, I ran my finger over the worn shelves and tables, surprised to see that nearly nothing inside had changed. I wandered from room to room. Stopping in the kitchen, I was relieved to see the cleaning service had indeed come and taken out the trash. I swung the fridge door open, discovering they had cleaned it out too. They'd left a few essentials and unopened packages. Eggs, butter, milk, cheese. There were no random leftovers like my mother was prone to keep. Unless that had changed.

I paused with my hand on the door, my eye caught on a photo slipped under one of the magnets. My mother and Aunt Clara, standing with their arms wrapped over each other's shoulder. And me—when I couldn't have been more than two or three years old, big toothy grin, perched on my mother's hip.

The number of years I'd missed my mother were almost as many as I'd had with her. I'd had a lot of time and distance to detach. Yet being here, seeing how little and how much could have changed all at the same time—was crushing. Some part of me had pictured everything back in Bleeding Valley Hearts unchanged. My mother and her house and all of her habits, just as I'd last seen them.

As if drawn by an invisible force, I continued my self tour through the house.

The house was eerily quiet. I bypassed my parents' bedroom—the door was closed, and I wasn't ready to go in there yet. I headed up the set of stairs to the small loft and bedroom upstairs. My old bedroom. The stairwell seemed darker than normal, and each step creaked loudly under my weight.

At the top of the stairs, the loft area was unchanged. Running a finger over my old bookshelf, I could tell my mother had still been cleaning up here—minimal dust. My desk sat next to the shelf, it all looked exactly as I had left it. The paperback novels I'd loved in high school lined the bookshelf. A small shoebox of memorabilia sat on the floor under my desk. I barely remembered what was in there, but I'd explore that later.

Two doors opened off the loft area—one to my bedroom, which was closed, and the other door, which was wide open, led to a tiny bathroom—barely big enough for the toilet, pedestal sink, and the triangular shaped corner shower that looked like a time-traveling portal.

Swinging open my bedroom door, it was like a shrine, untouched in all these years. Or at least as far as I could recall. My iron-frame bed took up most of the small room, still made up as though it would welcome me home at any time. *What a farce.* A beam of sun shone in from the parted curtains, so I hadn't bothered with the light switch.

My little nightstand with the teddy bear lamp I'd had my whole life was next to it, and I wondered if my mother had cleaned out the drawer. My heavy oak dresser towered in the corner, nicknacks and a small jewelry box on top. A small vanity table and stool across from my bed completed the room. My old makeup and nail polish were still on the vanity. My hairbrush, full of hair, sat on top of it, looking untouched. But I knew better because there wasn't more than a couple of weeks' worth of dust on the surfaces. *Why had my mom kept my room exactly as I'd left it, yet still wouldn't let me come home?* It made little sense.

Suddenly the room was spinning, a dizziness I couldn't explain overwhelming my body. I quickly sat down on the bed, the room swaying in my vision. The smell of lilacs filled my nostrils; there was a heaviness in my chest before everything went black.

"Patrick, stop, you're hurting me!" my mom cried.

Dad was drunk again, and mad at Mom for overcooking dinner. It wasn't even burnt. I didn't know what his problem was. Crouching in the corner of the living room, I looked over at the coffee table, littered with empty beer cans. Scratch that, I did know what his problem was.

"Dad, stop! You're going to break her arm!" I whimpered. Dad paused and looked at me, clutching my mother's arm behind her back. "Please, Daddy," I begged.

"You're going to be next if you don't mind your damn business, Grace," Dad spat at me, and I shriveled into myself.

"Grace, go upstairs," my mother hissed at me, and I hesitated for a moment. I should help her, but Dad scared the crap out of me when he was like this. Besides, what could I do?

"That's right, you whore; at least tell your daughter to mind her business." My father's words cut through my chest like a knife splitting me open.

I scrambled out of the corner and up the stairs to my bedroom. Closing the door as silently as I could, I suddenly wished there was a lock on it. Pulling my headphones on, I slipped under my comforter and blasted music in my ears as I burrowed into my pillows, tears streaming down my face. Occasionally there'd be a loud crash or the sound of objects breaking.

Huddled in bed, I debated calling Aunt Clara. She knew what my dad was like—I'd overheard her confronting him on more than one occasion. She would try to come to the rescue, but that would make it worse for my mom the next time.

And who knew? Maybe this time, he would take it all out on me? No, it was better not to involve other people.

It felt like forever before I felt, more than heard, the front door slam, the walls and windows vibrating from the force. Pulling my headphones off, I listened until I heard the familiar roar of my dad's truck engine as he peeled out of the driveway. The muffled sounds of my mother crying seemed to trickle up through the ceiling, each sniff tightening a knot in my chest.

Slipping out of my bed, I tiptoed to my door and opened it as quietly as I could, but the hinges squeaked, betraying me.

"It's okay, Grace," my mother called out softly. I hesitated for a moment before rushing downstairs.

Mom was lying on the couch, clutching her arm to her, fingerprint bruises already showing on her forearm. A glaring red welt on her cheek told me there would be a bruise there soon too. A quick surveillance of the room told me my dad had broken at least one of my mom's beloved antique figurines. Gifts passed down from her great-great grandmother, generation to generation, and my dad had smashed them in a fit of rage.

Scooping up one I thought was salvageable, I searched for the head that had broken off. Setting those two pieces on the side table, I grabbed the broom and dustpan to sweep up the shattered pieces of whatever else he had broken. After I swept those up, I grabbed a trash bag and dumped it all in and then angrily crushed and threw his beer cans in.

"Thank you, Gracey, you're such a good girl," my mom said, leaning back on the couch pillows, looking more defeated than I'd ever seen her. She usually fought back—or at least tried to protect herself. Why had today been different?

When I came to, the darkness was all wrong—too heavy, too complete. My head throbbed as I tried to determine how long I'd been out, but the blackness pressed in, swallowing any sense of time. Had I passed out again, or had I fallen asleep? The taste of the dream still clung to me—bitter, salty, like tears and mucus in the back of my throat. My stomach churned. It hadn't felt like a dream at all. More like a memory I'd lived through once before—and tried to forget.

Finding the light switch at the top of the landing, I made my way back downstairs. I'd lost the rest of the day—the biggest block of time I'd ever lost.

Toting my bags in from the car, I dropped them in the living room. Although I'd spent the whole day in bed, I found myself overwhelmed by exhaustion.

I scrounged around in the kitchen, trying to make a

meal for myself. I found a packet of tuna fish, some crackers and a small can of mandarin oranges. My pathetic meal seemed fitting. I stared down at the plate, wishing I had mayonnaise to mix with the tuna fish. The meal was so dry, I found myself gulping down water after each bite. After scarfing it down, I dragged my bags up to my bedroom, and flopped the one with all my clothing open.

I dug in my bag for my comfy pajamas. I longed to be wrapped in the softest material, cradled in my old bed. Despite the terrible memories flooding in, there was a deep ache inside me that wanted to lie in bed and sob for the mom I needed. The mom I missed. Maybe the mom I never really had.

CHAPTER FIVE

MORNING ARRIVED like a slap to the face, the sun shining through the window—more cheerful than anything should be, given the circumstances. I pushed the covers off me and swung my feet over to the edge of the bed.

After a pit-stop in the bathroom where I refused to look at my reflection, I made my way downstairs. I had never been so relieved in my life to dig up coffee in the kitchen. Silently thanking my mother for at least not switching to decaf over the years, I brewed a pot and pulled out an oversized mug. The milk in the fridge was expired, but there was always sugar to make the coffee palatable.

With a full mug, I glanced out the sliding doors to the backyard. I was surprised to see a small crabapple tree just outside the doors. Lilac bushes grew along the fence, and a large flower bed overflowing with beautiful plants grew at the back of the house. Intrigued, I walked over to the sliding doors and slid them open.

Our backyard had never looked like this. Growing up, the grass had been patchy, rarely mowed, but rarely needing it. There had been no intentional planting. I was thrown off, because my mother's beautiful backyard did not align with the house's condition.

A small framed hammock chair rested under that tree, and I made my way over, carefully lowering myself into it, not wanting to spill hot coffee on myself. My head barely cleared the low branches of the small tree, but I leaned back and relaxed into the fabric, letting myself sway under the tree.

For a moment, I let myself feel grateful for being here in the late spring, with everything in bloom. I didn't know when the backyard became so beautiful and relaxing, but it calmed my soul. There was an almost eeriness about the calmness in the late morning.

"Is that you, Grace Jenkins?" A voice on the other side of the fence made me jump, and coffee sloshed out of my mug onto my thighs. Grumbling, I wiped it off, standing up out of the chair.

"Umm, Mrs. Paulson?" I responded, not looking forward to having a conversation with the neighbor. She had always been nosy and overbearing—butting her nose in when she shouldn't—making it hard to keep our little family secret. But I couldn't ignore her and go inside and close the door, like I wanted to. *Could I?*

"Yes, but you're a grown lady now, Grace, you can call me Dotty," she answered, her eyes suddenly peeking over a small broken part of the fence. I wondered if she had broken it to spy, because the rest of the fence was in impeccable condition. It had definitely been replaced since I had been gone.

"Oh, sure... Dotty," I respond weakly, not having anything to say to this woman whom I'd avoided as a teenager.

"I'm so sorry about your mama—I'm the one who found her, you know? If there's anything I can do..."

"Oh, thank you—and thank you for calling... for help for her..." I trailed off, not sure what to say.

"When is the funeral going to be, dear? Ralph and I would like to attend and pay our respects."

"Oh, I don't think I'll be having one—we don't have any other family here, and she's being..." I paused, feeling strange telling my neighbor this—or rather, saying it out loud for the first time. "...cremated."

"Oh dear. That's too bad." Dotty made a tutting sound, something between pity and judgment. My chest tightened, and I opened my mouth, but no response came. Dotty barrelled on, filling the silence. "Well, you let me know if I can do anything for you at all, dearie. Heidi has been so private—you know she rarely left the house—always tending her garden in the backyard. I wondered why you didn't come around to visit. It's been years. And her all alone after your father..." Dotty was fishing for information, but I didn't have answers for her. I didn't even have answers for myself.

"Yeah..." I left the unspoken question hanging in the air between us. Dotty stood watching me, waiting for me to say more. Finally, she let out a loud harrumph, giving up.

"I'll check in with you later. I'll bring you a casserole."

"Oh, that's not necessary. Very sweet, but you don't have to cook for me." *Please don't. Don't come knocking on the door and try to push your way in.*

"I insist, and I won't take no for an answer. It can be hard to remember to eat when you're grieving. Let me drop it by tonight," she said and with a wave, she was gone before I could protest.

The neighbor's words left me reeling. *That's too bad?* Was it weird I was having my mother cremated and didn't plan on having any funeral or service? The question kept echoing in my head long after the conversation ended, like a sound that wouldn't quite fade. Was I being callous, disrespectful or even cold? I tried to tell myself it was practical—simple, clean—but now I wasn't so sure. I didn't even know who would come if I did plan a memorial service. Who would I invite? Who still remembered her?

My mother had kept to herself even when I was a kid —quiet, withdrawn, always turning down neighbors' offers or invitations—and it sounded like not much had changed. Maybe no one would show up. I'd end up sitting in an empty pew, pretending not to notice the rows of unfilled seats.

Even though I knew those things, the thought of doing nothing at all made my stomach twist. It felt wrong in a way I couldn't name, like I was forgetting an invisible rule about grief that everyone else seemed to know instinctively. People had funerals. People said goodbye. What kind of person didn't?

But every time I imagined hosting one—having to write a eulogy, ordering flowers, choosing music—I froze. What would I even say about her? *My mother told me not to come home. She refused to talk to me for the last thirteen years. But here I am, ha! Mom.* The idea of standing there, speaking as if I understood her, or even knew her anymore, would be a big fat lie.

I didn't even know if my mom had a service for my father. Right after he disappeared into Moon Lake—that's when Mom cut me off. Heartbroken to be alone for Christmas, I had searched for answers. At the time, I wondered if she didn't want me dealing with the gossipy neighbors—the knowing stares. After all, we could be fairly sure good ole' Dad had been drunk when he drove into the lake. But she never called me home for a funeral—she never let me come home again.

Acknowledging all of this didn't dispel the doubts, though—I couldn't shake the neighbor's tone, the tiny pause before she said, "Oh dear..." judgment ringing in her response. Who knew, maybe she was right. There was a good chance I was doing this completely wrong.

CHAPTER SIX

WANDERING THROUGH THE HOUSE, I stopped in the living room and looked at my mom's prized antique figurines. The shelf they were on, once overflowed with the porcelain ladies, now had only a few left. I remembered examining each of those ladies, the details on their dresses, and wishing I could play with them like dolls when I was probably five or six years old.

Gradually, those ladies had gotten broken, one by one. The occasional doll got bumped by accident, many at the hands of my angry father—knowing how much my mother cherished them. I didn't know why she never packed them up and put them away to keep them safe.

Reaching out, I lifted the one I remembered gluing the head back on. I ran my finger around the crack in her neck, and chills raced up my spine. I froze, the air around me suddenly colder. Then, from deeper in the house, a soft creak answered my thoughts. It wasn't the pipes or the wind—it was deliberate, like a footstep on an old floorboard. I held my breath. The doll's shiny eyes caught the light, staring past me, toward the hallway that led to

Mom's bedroom. Was I being watched? I looked around behind me.

For a moment, I tried to laugh it off—just nerves, just the house settling, just memory playing tricks.

"Mom?" I said out loud, and turned around to look. Part of me expected to find her standing there smiling at me, arms open for me to fall into. But there was no one else there. Just me and my own thoughts creeping me out.

You're an idiot. Mom wouldn't talk to you when she's alive; she's certainly not going to break her silence now, I chastised myself, but I couldn't shake the feeling of being watched. It was definitely being back in this house I'd grown up in —scared to set off my father most evenings, I'd spent the majority of my time in my bedroom.

I turned back to survey the rest of the room. My mom didn't have many personal belongings in the living room —a few framed photos on the mantel, a stack of old magazines, the afghan she crocheted years ago draped neatly over the arm of the couch. Everything was in its place, as if she'd stepped out for a quick minute. Packing this place up should be easy, I told myself. A few boxes and tape. It was just stuff.

But then my eyes drifted toward the hallway—toward her bedroom door, still closed. I couldn't bring myself to check it out. The thought alone made my chest tighten. It wasn't merely a room; it was *her*. Her scent would still be in the air, faint but unmistakable. Her slippers might still be beside the bed. The dent in the pillow where her head used to rest. All those traces of a life that had simply stopped.

The moment I turned that doorknob, it would all become real in a way it hadn't yet. The house still felt like she was in it—maybe folding laundry, maybe humming to herself in the kitchen. Opening the door would shatter every illusion. Maybe I was being a big baby, but I couldn't do it yet. Not today. Not while the room still felt like it was holding the key to unlock the door I'd closed so long ago inside me.

The shelf rattled behind me, the figurines clinking, as a big truck barreled by on the road. I'd forgotten these little quirks about the house, and it startled me. I paused for a moment, watching the figurines settle into place. I couldn't let every little sound spook me.

Grabbing my laptop bag from the floor where I'd left it yesterday so I could check in with work and see if there were any important contracts in need of my attention, I set up a workstation at the table.

I didn't even know if my mother had Wi-Fi—did she even *use* the internet? When I was a kid, she said she'd never had any reason to. "If I need information, I'll look it up at the library or ask around," she used to say, as if Google were a nosy neighbor she had no interest in talking to. She wrote everything down in a little spiral notebook by the phone—numbers, recipes, birthdays—her own version of a search engine. I could almost picture her now, sitting at the kitchen table with a cup of instant coffee, frowning at a blinking router light like it was judging her.

A quick check told me there was definitely no internet here. And since the hot spot on my phone never functioned right, I was going to have to check my work email from my phone and let them know I was flat out of work until I could at least get internet access set up.

Once I finished, I called and arranged for service to be hooked up. I did it without thinking. While I was saving the appointment in my phone's calendar, the customer service rep long gone, I paused. Why did I schedule internet service to be hooked up? *How long did I think I would be here, anyway?* The house needed a decent amount of work before I could sell it. And I still hadn't decided on renting it out or selling it. So either way, I figured I'd go ahead with the appointment. I couldn't be here for *weeks* without internet service.

Stop talking yourself in circles. Who cares anyway? If you only stay three weeks, you can cancel the service when you leave.

Resigned to not being able to get much work done, I poked around the kitchen cabinets. My mother was prone to keeping things—empty butter dishes, random takeout containers, claiming they could be useful. I figured if nothing else, I could accomplish one task and feel productive, so I dug around under the kitchen sink and found the trash bags. Shaking one open, I got busy throwing away all these useless containers.

The doorbell startled me. It sounded too loud in the quiet of my mother's house, echoing through rooms. The afternoon had passed me by. I pushed past the three trash bags I'd filled and made my way to the front door. I'd forgotten about the neighbor stopping by.

When I opened the door, Dotty stood there, clutching a glass casserole dish wrapped in foil and wearing the same expression as earlier—half sympathy, half busybody.

"Oh, Grace," she said, drawing the word out. "You look a sight. I know you must be having a time over here, all alone."

She pushed the dish toward me before I could protest. It was warm. "Chicken and rice," she added. "Comfort food. You look like you could use a good meal."

"Thank you, Mrs. Paulson," I said automatically. I wished she would drop off the food and go away, but no such luck. "I'll be sure to wash and return this dish to you when I'm done."

"Oh, dear, please call me Dotty. Everyone does." She tilted her head and frowned, counting back the years. "Must be what, ten? Maybe twelve years?" I lifted an eyebrow, wondering what she was blathering on about. "Since I last saw you here," she said, again with the judgmental tone.

"Sounds about right." I stepped aside to let her in, realizing I didn't have a choice at this point. I didn't want her to come in, but old habits die hard—Dotty never had waited for an invitation anyway. Some things never change. Even when everything else had.

She shuffled past me, her eyes darting around the living room like she was taking inventory. "Heidi sure kept a neat house. Always did. Though she never had much company."

"I know."

"I used to tell her she ought to have people over once in a while," Dotty went on, peering at the mantel, the tidy shelves. She paused at the figurines. "But she said she didn't see the point. 'I don't need anyone else in my house, Dotty,' she'd say. 'I've got all I need.'" It sounded exactly like my mom.

She laughed lightly, though it wasn't a happy sound. "Guess she was always a private one. Not like your aunt… Clara, wasn't it?"

At the mention of my aunt, my stomach twisted. "You knew Aunt Clara?"

"Oh, sure. In a way—or in passing, at least. Your mother and her had a falling out, though. Terrible fights, they had. I hate to bring it up at a time like this, but I did have to call the police once... Or maybe twice?" She looked at me expectantly, as though I had the answers, but I was even more in the dark than her.

I didn't want to let on how clueless I was, but how else was I going to find out what was going on?

"What do you mean?" I asked as nonchalantly as possible. The casserole was probably getting heavy, so I waved for her to follow me into the kitchen so I could set it down. The smell wafted up, and my stomach grumbled.

"Well," she began, settling herself down at the kitchen table, "why don't you fix yourself a plate, and I'll tell you? I heard your stomach growl." She laughed, and made herself comfortable, like a cat finding its perch.

"You don't mind? I am starving, actually. And this does smell delicious—I appreciate it so much," I praised, probably the most sincere thing I'd said to her all day.

"Not at all, dear. You need to eat."

"Would you like to eat with me? Or can I get you a drink?"

"Oh, no, I ate with Ralph. I'm fine." She waved me away, and I grabbed a spoon and dished out a big plate for myself. Grabbing a fork and a glass of water, I plopped down at the kitchen table across from her.

"So." I paused between bites, fighting back the urge to moan as the food hit my stomach. "They had a fight?"

"Oh yes, many fights, I think. Most of the time it was screaming, so I didn't worry too much. Sisters, prone to fighting, I supposed? But I was out on the porch one night —shortly before Christmas that year, I think it was—and I heard shouting. Women's voices, angry. Things crashing. I could see through the curtains, Clara was here, waving her arms around. Heidi was crying. Next thing I know, I heard glass break, and I thought, well, I can't sit here and let them hurt each other, can I? So I called it in."

Dotty took a breath, clearly satisfied with her memory. "Two officers came. But by the time they got here, everything was quiet. I guess they'd calmed down. But one of the officers escorted Clara to her car. It wasn't long afterwards… I stopped seeing Clara come around at all."

I hadn't realized I'd started tearing up until one rolled down my cheek and Dotty reached out to pat my hand.

"Oh dear, I don't want to upset you. Heidi never seemed the same after what happened to your father. And then after Clara, she was… not herself. You know how a person can look at you, but you can tell they're seeing something else? That was her. Every time I stopped by with pie or for a chat, she'd be polite, but she'd be… far away. Like her mind was in a place I couldn't follow."

Dotty smoothed her dress, avoiding my eyes. "I figured maybe she felt guilty. Sisters fight, you know. We say things we don't mean."

Her words hung in the air. I thought about my mother sitting alone here for all those years, never having Aunt Clara here, never inviting me home. Her and this house. It was like they had become one thing.

Dotty stood again, peering toward the hallway. "Did you go through her room yet?"

"No," I said quickly. *What a weird question, Dotty.* I knew she must have driven Mom crazy with her nosiness.

"Mmm. Probably for the best, for now. She didn't like people to go in there anyway. Always kept the door closed. I asked her once why, and she said she couldn't stand drafts. But all rooms need to be aired out. Like our dirty laundry," she said pointedly. I was pretty sure it was the opposite—we weren't supposed to air our dirty laundry, but I was sure Dotty was a sucker for the drama that ensued when anyone did.

A silence settled between us, thick and uncomfortable. Dotty cleared her throat. "Anyway. I'll get out of your hair. You've got enough to handle. But if you need anything, you know where I am—same place as always. I'll see myself out." She waved her hand, signaling for me not to get up.

She patted my arm, already making her way out. However, she hesitated at the doorway. "Oh, and if you hear any… noises at night, don't be alarmed. Old houses like this—they remember things. The walls settle, the pipes groan, creaking. It's the house talking."

I tried to smile, but it came out wrong. "Thanks, Dotty." *And what the fuck, Dotty? Why are you trying to creep me out? What an old biddy.*

After she left, I sat there, staring down at my plate. I'd nearly finished the large serving, but the emptiness inside me blossomed and grew until I found myself eating the casserole directly out of the dish, bite after bite. I desperately wanted to fill the gaping hole—the emptiness my mother had left so long ago, but I couldn't.

The house felt even emptier than before Dotty's visit. I'd have thought I would be grateful to see her go, but I would have traded feeling so alone with her yappy gossip anyday.

I walked back into the living room and looked toward the closed bedroom door. Dotty's voice echoed in my head *—didn't like people to go in there… never the same after Clara… it's the house talking.*

The bedroom door at the end of the hall looked the same as it always had—white paint, brass knob, slightly chipped at the edge. I took a step toward it, then stopped.

A faint shift of floorboards on the other side.

Maybe the house was settling. Like Dotty said

Maybe not.

Outside, I thought I heard footsteps again—or maybe it was Dotty's voice, faintly, carrying across the yard. But when I went to the window, her porch light was off, and her house was dark.

And from down the hall, behind her closed door, I could swear I heard a soft, deliberate creak—like weight on the floorboards, waiting.

INCIDENT REPORT

Case Number: 25-15891

Date/Time: 12/13/2014 - 20:45 PM

Location: 518 Monmouth Drive

Type of Incident: Possible Domestic Disturbance

Reporting Officer: Ofc. L. Duley #168

Summary:

At approximately 20:45 PM hours, this officer was dispatched to 518 Monmouth Drive in reference to a report of a possible domestic disturbance. The call was made by a neighbor (later identified as Dorothy Paulson), who reported hearing yelling and what sounded like items being thrown inside the residence.

Upon arrival at 21:02 PM, I observed the residence to be dark except for a light in a front window. I knocked on the front door and announced my presence as law enforcement. After approximately 30 seconds, the door was opened by a female later identified as **[Heidi Jenkins]**. The subject appeared visibly upset and stated that she had been arguing with her sister, **[Clara Miller]**.

The sister was located inside the residence. Both parties denied any physical altercation, stating that the argument had been verbal only. I observed no visible injuries on either individual. Several household items (a picture frame and a small lamp) were found knocked over in the living room area. The sister was still mumbling about a disagreement over the garden. The resident states her sister is mentally unwell and she is looking at options for residential care currently.

The sister agreed to leave the residence without incident.

No arrests were made at this time. Both parties were advised of resources and provided contact information for local support services.

Case Status: Closed (Verbal Disturbance Only)

Officer's Signature: L Duley. Ofc #168

/ s / Ofc. L. Duley #168

Bleeding Hearts Valley Police Department

CHAPTER SEVEN

IF I HAD BEEN AVOIDING thoughts of my mother all these years, then I had built an even stronger wall around the subject of my father. His name alone carried a kind of static in my chest—a discomfort I couldn't name. His disappearance had been a strange mixture of grief and relief, like a wound that hurt but also eased a deeper ache. I was sure everyone in town whispered about it with pity and speculation, but I remember feeling mostly numb.

Maybe because part of me had been expecting it. Maybe because part of me thought it was the only way his story could ever end. Still, his absence didn't set me free the way I once imagined it might.

The night they dragged his truck from Moon Lake, it was as though the last fragile thread tying me to home had snapped. Maybe the shame was why I wasn't allowed back home.

I couldn't shake the question of what my mother had been avoiding all those years. She was good at silence, at pretending not talking about a problem would make it disappear. Maybe I learned it from her—the art of burying things deep enough you almost forget they exist. Still, the mind had its own way of unearthing what had been buried.

The questions crept into my dreams, warping into uneasy shapes. I'd wake in the middle of the night drenched in sweat, heart pounding, certain something—or someone—was trying to surface. It was strange how memory worked, how it waited until you came home to start haunting you again.

Being back in this place felt like stepping into another life entirely, one that still existed beneath the surface of the present. The smells, the light, the rhythm of the wind against the windows—they all carried traces of who I used to be. I'd worked so hard to stamp down those memories, to build new ones on top of them, but now they come rushing back in floods and fragments.

It was as though the past had been waiting for me here, patient and silent, knowing I'd eventually have to face it.

I woke up feeling like I hadn't slept in days. I wasn't thinking straight, and in a brain fog, I decided to make a morning trip to Moon Lake. I didn't know what I was hoping for—seeing where my dad's truck had driven over the edge into the depths of the lake—maybe it would give me closure.

I got dressed and dug around the kitchen for a travel mug. Filling it with coffee, I resolved to go to the grocery store today. I was desperate for the sweet dose of creamer my coffee badly needed.

Backing out of the driveway, I made my way out of the neighborhood, suddenly noticing how run-down the outside of the house was compared to the other houses on the street. Bad was an understatement—it was atrocious. Dirty windows, screens with holes, loose shutters, dirty siding. The list of things that hadn't been cared for was endless.

Hopping on Main Street, I zipped across town.

The road to Moon Lake hadn't changed much since that night. The same narrow, cracked asphalt wound through the trees like a black vein. Pines leaned close, whispering in the damp air, their needles glistening. I drove with the window cracked, letting in the smell of wet earth and the faint tang of rain.

When I reached the clearing, the lake spread before me like a sheet of dull glass, gray and motionless under a low ceiling of early morning clouds. An old boat ramp was still there, though half-swallowed by moss and mud. I parked near it and killed the engine. For a long moment, I sat, listening to the tick of the car settling.

This was where they pulled his truck from the water. Where the searchlights cut through the night and reflected off the rain.

Where my father's story ended. An end that everyone had expected.

He'd been drinking. Everyone knew it. That night had been another in a long string of bad nights—his voice slurred, eyes glassy, temper flaring like a struck match. An 'accident.' I'd repeated that word to myself for years until it became a mantra. But the older I got, the less the word fit.

I stepped out of the car, my sneakers sinking into the mud. The air was colder than I expected, sharp against my skin. A breeze came off the lake, brushing against the trees, and I could almost hear his laugh carried in it—a low, rough sound. It had once put fear in me. His laugh was never a happy laugh full of joy. It was an angry bark, full of contempt.

I sat on the edge of the dock, letting my legs dangle over the water. The surface barely rippled, holding its secrets close. I tried to think, to remember clearly, but the past always came in fragments: the sound of the truck engine, the slam of its door, and rain hammering the roof. My own voice, smaller then, shouting, although I couldn't recall what.

The world spun on its axis, and the smell of lilacs overwhelmed me—almost suffocating in the damp air. The smell grew stronger, filling my head until it drowned everything else. The earthy scent of the lake disappeared under that sickening sweet lilac scent. My pulse quickened. I tried to stand, but the ground shifted under me, the dock fading into gray light, and then—nothing.

When I came to, I was standing outside. Where was I? Rain was falling hard—sheets of it. The lake was darker, swollen and wild.

Flashes—too quick to hold onto.

Headlights cutting through mist.

Mud sucking at my shoes.

A splash.

A voice whisper-shouting. Was that Aunt Clara?

My mother telling me to stop crying.

The cold seeped through my clothes, biting into my bones. My heart hammered, and for a moment I could almost see him—his outline by the driver's door, his face turned toward me. There was something in his expression… not anger, not fear, but sorrow. Then it all blurred again.

The sound of the rain roared in my ears, the lilacs faded, and I was back on the boat dock, shivering, breath clouding in the air. The lake was calm again. Quiet, as if nothing had ever happened.

I stared out over the water, unsure if what I'd seen was a memory or dream. But buried deep down, a truth was rising to the surface—slow, inevitable.

Maybe my father hadn't driven into the lake.

Maybe the lake was trying to send me a message. The answers weren't here at the lake, and I was overcome with exhaustion. I needed a nap, so I headed back home. *Home* was such a weird way to think about a house when it wasn't my home anymore and hadn't been for so long. But once, so long ago, it had been. And it was again—at least for right now.

CHAPTER EIGHT

AFTER A MUCH NEEDED NAP, I made a quick run to the grocery store to stop and pick up packing supplies. It was a relief to make a cup of coffee the way I liked it, and to eat fresh food. I felt more refreshed and determined and decided today was the day I would go in my mother's bedroom. I needed to assess how much work there would be in there.

Dragging the packing boxes and tape, a trash bag dangling from one wrist down the hall, I paused at her door. I stood there listening, expecting to hear my parents arguing. Or my dad's drunken snores. The brass doorknob caught a beam of afternoon sunlight, glinting like an eye that knew I would eventually have to turn it. But each time I reached for it, something in me recoiled, as though the air on the other side would be too heavy to breathe.

Before I could think of another excuse, I sucked in my breath and turned the knob, letting the door fall open. The smell hit me first—floral and another scent—older and softer. My mother. It felt like she'd barely left the room, like she'd walk back in any moment, humming under her breath, her slippers whispering against the carpet. The illusion was so strong, I almost called to her again. Instead, I stood still, clutching the boxes, and let my eyes adjust to the dim light filtering through lace curtains.

Everything appeared to be exactly as she had left it. Bed, neatly made, a frayed throw blanket folded at the foot, and the indentation on her pillow still showing exactly where she had rested her head. A pair of reading glasses—a new addition to who my mother had been now —rested on the nightstand on a stack of romance novels, the top one half-read, with a bookmark marking her spot.

My pulse throbbed in my ears, and I gave myself a moment to close my eyes and just breathe. Dropping my supplies on the bed, I gave myself a pep talk. I wasn't in this room to mourn or think about all of the details about my mother. I was here to take stock, and to see what needed to be packed up or thrown away.

The logical part of me kept reiterating this thought, while my impulse else fought against it, the air in the room weighing those thoughts down. Everything in this room was full of memories—most of them not mine.

I started with her dresser—it seemed like the easiest since I didn't need to keep her clothes. The top was covered with lotions, creams, and perfumes. My mother was a simple woman, but she always took care of her skin and she had an affinity for perfumes. The collection she had amassed was overwhelming.

Opening the trash bag, I tossed in the lotions and creams, her deodorant and nail polish without a passing thought. I paused at the perfumes, the glass bottles gleaming like little shrines. I recognized several of the bottles from my childhood—either tried and true scents she bought on repeat, or bottles she hoarded, rarely ever using.

My mother believed the perfect scent could turn your day around. She wore these perfumes like a coat of armor. They gave the perception she was all soft and floral… when inside, she was steel.

I flicked through the bottles, tossing them gently into the trash. Ones I didn't recognize or didn't care for—I was not a perfume-person. I liked my scents more subtle and fresh. Moving a big bottle I didn't recognize into the trash bag, there I saw it… the bottle of lilac perfume—her signature scent. The bottle was a vintage design, a small lavender tinted vial with a rose gold cap. I didn't need to open it to smell it. It had followed her everywhere, and lingered long after she'd left a room. I'd never forget it. It still haunted me.

For a second, it was like she was there with me in the room, standing at the dresser, offering me a spritz, dabbing a drop behind my ear. I set the bottle aside gently. I couldn't bring myself to throw that one away. The rest I swept off into the trash one by one, the glass clinking in the bag, breaking the silence of the room.

Once I was done with the top of the dresser, I moved on to the drawers. Those were easier—my mom had a simple wardrobe with basic blouses and pants hung in the closet so the dresser had a few pairs of pajamas, socks, underwear, and bras. I threw all of the clothes into a box to donate, and turned to the closet, a burst of energy suddenly pushing me to get things done. Opening the closet doors, I pushed aside the rows and rows of slacks, blouses, and dresses. I paused when I realized my father's work clothes were all still hanging in the closet. Lifting out one of his old work shirts, I wondered—why had my mother hung onto these things?

But touching these clothes was like poison, memories flooding over me. In a flurry, I ripped them out of the closet, throwing them into the box haphazardly. Then I moved on to my mother's clothes, less rushed. I ran my thumb over a cardigan—I couldn't believe she still had this after all those years. Aunt Clara had taken me shopping to pick it out for her for Christmas one year. I couldn't have been more than five—it was my first time choosing a gift and I'd been so proud of myself.

Pushing that cardigan to the back of the closet, I slipped the rest of the clothes into the donation box. The room was starting to feel claustrophobic, like all the air had been sucked out of it. I turned away from the closet, desperate for a distraction. Less personal items.

I slipped into the chair of her vanity, dragging the trash bag with me. Tossing her brush and a few basic makeup items into the bag, I pulled out the drawer. A small jewelry box lay in the drawer and I paused, fingers on the lid.

My mother was never a jewelry wearer. She'd worn a plain wedding band, and nothing else. Lifting the lid, I inspected the bracelet lying inside. I lifted it out and turned it around in my hands. I was no expert, but this was definitely a decent piece of jewelry. I wondered who had given it to her, because one thing I knew for sure was it wasn't my father.

My foot bumped against something under the vanity and I slid the chair back out to see what it was. Looking under, I was surprised to see a small worn wooden chest. It had big brass hinges, with a lock hanging open. I wondered what on earth my mother could have in there.

Sliding down onto the floor, I pulled it out in front of

me. The weight of it surprised me—whatever was in the box was a lot heavier than I'd expected.

I lifted the lid and the scent of old paper and books hit me, like when you enter the library. The box was full of stacks of envelopes—stacks banded together—many loose cards, notes, and several journals breaking at the seams, clearly full to the brim. My mother's loopy handwriting was on most of the envelopes but I also recognized my aunt's handwriting and my own on several card envelopes.

Thumbing through the first stack, I read through several birthday cards I'd given her when I was little. Drawings—little notes I'd written. She had kept them all. In between the cards, little notes and photos occasionally fell out. Lifting one, I smiled at the memory. My seventh birthday—my mom had made me a big pink cake. It was a birthday my father hadn't been able to ruin because he had been stuck working late.

I swallowed hard as I lifted out one of the journals. Flipping through the pages, I imagined her curled up with a pen, filling page after page with her thoughts and memories. Occasionally I paused to read a couple of lines. It felt vaguely invasive, but I hadn't run across anything overtly personal yet. This particular journal seemed to be a bunch of notes about her backyard garden.

Picking up another journal, an envelope fluttered out of the pages to the floor. I picked it up, examining the outside. My mother's handwriting in a name on the front. *Phillip.* No address, no stamp or postmark. It wasn't sealed, so I slipped it open and pulled out the singular piece of paper. The scent of lilacs bloomed out.

The letter itself was a bit cryptic. I didn't know who Phillip was, but it sounded like my mother had known him well. I read through it several times—it wasn't dated —and it left me with a list of unanswered questions. *Why would she have a letter that she wrote?*

Glancing back at the box, I wondered what else it held. What secrets did my mom have stored here? So many letters—my pulse quickened at the thought of what my mother might have been hiding all those years.

I reached out my hand to pick up another, but before I could, a sound ripped me out of my thoughts—knocking at the door. *Dammit Dotty.* I pulled myself off the floor, brushing dust off my pants.

Another knock, and I was ready to snap. She was so impatient!

"Coming!" I called, rushing out to the front door.

Dearest Phillip,

I don't know where to start this letter- how to put into words all the things I'd like to say to you.

I wanted to tell you how much I appreciate all you have done. I don't know how I would have ever made it through this investigation without your help. I'm sorry you ever had to step in.

You were right about so many things- there's a heaviness in my heart for all I have lost. And I have nothing but deep deep sorrow for any pain or troubles I have caused you.

No one in my life has ever gone out of their way for me the way you have- and for that I will be eternally grateful.

This is not the closure I wanted- this is not the ending I wanted. I hope you live a beautiful life for many years to come and find all the happiness I truly feel you deserve.

With all of my heart,
Love, Heidi

CHAPTER NINE

I SWUNG THE DOOR OPEN, brushing my hair out of my face. But it wasn't Dotty. The man standing there must have been right around my age. He was wearing a button-down shirt and tie, and carried a clipboard pressed against his side. Tall and lanky, his dark hair slicked back, his wide spread eyes darted to me. Eyes like a weasel. He was grinning in that way only a door to door salesman ever could. A mixture of fakeness and hopefulness. But this guy had something else too—I couldn't put my finger on it, but there was a hint of something darker about him.

"Can I help you?" I asked, lifting an eyebrow. I wanted to flat out tell him my mother recently died and I wasn't prepared to buy anything, but I couldn't get the words out.

"Hello. My name is Thomas Andrews, and I'm a realtor in the area. I noticed—well, I hate to be so frank, but I noticed this house had gotten a little run-down. So I've been looking into it—and I found out the homeowner had passed away. I'm so sorry for your loss..." He paused, having spewed his spiel all out in one breath.

"Already? How did you know already?" I asked.

"Oh, I'm sorry, Ms..." He waited for me to tell him who I was, but something about the way he said it made me think he already knew.

"Jenkins. This was my mother's house."

"Right, right. So, I work closely with a developer—and they're interested in this property. I heard through the good old rumor mill—you don't live in town? So I thought you might be interested in selling? Listen, I'm sorry to drop by this way, but... could I come in?" Thomas tipped his chin, and I glanced over my shoulder at the living room, as though expecting to see someone else there.

I still had the door open only halfway. I could say no. But I didn't. I didn't know why I didn't... but instead I turned and led the way into the house, regretting my decision with every step.

"Can I get you a glass of water?" I asked, my midwestern hospitality kicking in.

"No thanks, I'm good." I waved him toward the sofa and I perched on the edge of an armchair.

"So, like I was saying, I have a developer who's extremely interested, you could easily get top dollar for this property. Even in the condition it's currently in." Thomas flipped through the papers on his clipboard, the plastic cover crackling with each flip. I watched as a small piece of paper fluttered out and landed under the coffee table. He didn't seem to notice. I leaned forward, prepared to pick it up, but a sudden cold blast of air made my arm hairs stand on end. Like a warning *not* to pick it up.

"Top dollar, huh?" I said, sitting back slowly. "That's interesting, but... I don't think I'm planning to sell." The words slipped out before I had even decided on them. I wasn't sure why I said it—I hadn't thought about not selling at all, but now he was here pushing me to, it didn't sound right. The idea of giving up the place suddenly felt wrong. Deeply wrong.

Thomas's pen froze mid-scribble. His head tilted slightly, the polite-fake realtor's smile flattening into a tighter line. And there it was—that shadow of darkness again.

"Not planning to sell?" He repeated it like it was a foreign phrase. "You'd be passing up a very good offer. Honestly, you won't see numbers like this again for a long time." The words sounded like friendly persuasive advice, but the tone had a threatening edge to it.

"I appreciate that," I said, forcing a firmness in my tone even though it didn't match how I felt. "But it's not about the money."

He exhaled sharply through his nose and straightened his tie. "Not about the money," he echoed, his tone taking on an edge. "Look, I don't know what kind of sentimental attachment you've got here, but—" He looked around the room, and then pointedly at the front window. Standing, he pointed his pen out to the front of the house. "The amount of work needed on this house… it's in shambles."

"I said I'm not planning to sell," I interrupted, my voice steadier now. "That's all."

Thomas's jaw tightened. For a moment, I thought he might say something cutting—to remind me of how much I clearly didn't know about real estate. A comment that betrayed his fake polite persona. But then he blinked, forced a smile, and the tension seemed to melt from his shoulders. "Of course," he said lightly. "Of course, you've got to do what feels right for you. No pressure. I thought I'd make sure you were aware of your options."

He shuffled his papers back into his clipboard, the

motion quick and practiced. "Anyway, I've got a few more stops today. You think it over, and if you change your mind, you've got my number." He dropped his business card on the coffee table.

"I know you're in mourning. Must be hard to part with your mother's home. How about I stop by again in a few days? Give you a chance to think it over?" Thomas didn't wait for my answer. He turned and opened the door to let himself out.

"Thanks for giving me a chance to introduce myself. You have a great day, Grace." My heart thudded in my chest. I hadn't given him my first name. So he *did* know who I was. *Who was this guy?*

I nodded, keeping my expression neutral until he was out the door. The air was still again, too still. I waited until his vehicle pulled out of the driveway before I crouched down and peered under the coffee table as I contemplated how he'd used my first name when I hadn't given it to him. My hands shook as I reached for the paper. I know it was easy enough for him to have searched for my information—but it was unsettling for him to pretend he didn't know who I was when he clearly had.

The slip of paper was still there, curled at the edges because it had been handled a lot. I hesitated, feeling a strange cold twinge again, but this time I ignored it. Carefully, I pulled it out and examined it.

It was a rough sketch of a property—basic lines and measurements, faint notes scribbled along the borders. And there, plain as day, my mom's address was written in thick pencil, 518 Monmouth Drive. But the shape of the house… it wasn't at all right. It looked completely different. Whoever drew it was planning for changes that hadn't happened yet.

turn BACKYARD into COURTYARD

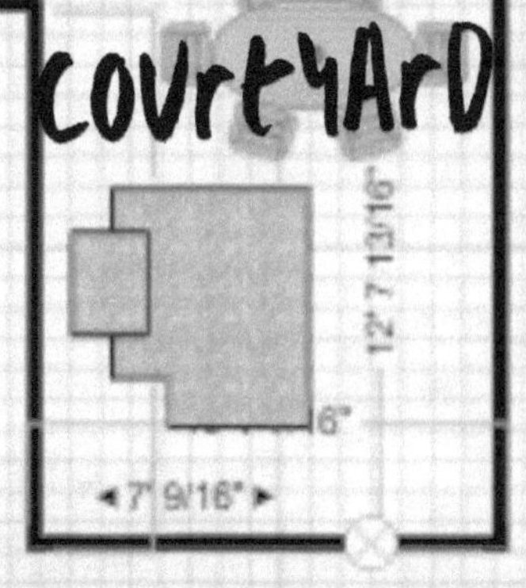

HAVE Jim DrAW UP PLANS for APArtment LAYOUT

~~HOUSE CUrrENTLY SET BACK~~ from rOAD, CAN MOVE UP

518 Monmouth Drive

CHAPTER TEN

I PARKED outside White Oak Manor, the sky threatening rain again. The clouds hovered low and heavy, as though waiting to burst open. I sat in the car for a few extra minutes, considering what I might say—allowing myself to imagine the way the conversation might go.

Guilt pricked at me, a little nudge in my chest, because I should have known Aunt Clara was staying here. All these years, and I'd had no clue. With a sigh, I stepped out of the car. The building loomed in front of me with its clean modern design—beige and white with a touch of pale sage. Hanging baskets of plants on the small porch gave a touch of tender care. The air smelled like rain and mud and cut grass, and as I got closer to the front door, a faint trickle of disinfectant—the unmistakable scent of hospital-level care.

Swinging into the small lobby, the warmth enveloped me, mixed with that sterile scent. The lobby was quiet aside from the receptionist tap-tapping away at her keyboard. She glanced up from her computer and smiled at me.

"Hello. I'm here to visit my aunt, Clara Miller."

"Oh hello, you must be Heidi's daughter." Her voice softened. "I'm so sorry, but Ms. Clara isn't taking visitors today."

"Not taking visitors? What does that mean?" My heart lurched, but I maintained a steady tone. "Is she sick?"

"Let me get a nurse who can speak with you." She stood and gestured toward the chairs in the waiting area. "Have a seat, please." And she whisked away into the back.

I sat down as instructed and waited, anxiously tapping a foot.

When the nurse arrived, her eyes were already making apologies before she even opened her mouth to speak. She had a calming presence, and she waved me back into a small room with a table and four chairs. I flopped into a chair without asking, but she remained standing.

"Is Aunt Clara alright?" I asked immediately, my stomach churning nervously. I'd expected this to be an unusual visit but now I was worried something was genuinely wrong. Aside from the obvious.

"I'm Nurse Eva, and I'm in charge of the shift today. I'm so sorry you came out today and won't be able to see her. Clara has had a rough couple of days."

"What do you mean? What's wrong with her?" The guilt in my chest tightened its grip.

She hesitated for a moment, and then sank down into the chair across from me, her eyes meeting mine.

"Yesterday, there was an incident. It's unfortunately been an issue for Clara all along. I… I'm not sure how much you know of her condition. But for Clara, the rain is a trigger—it sends her into a fit. And usually we try to keep her calm and busy—and mostly contained to her room during heavy rain. But yesterday she managed to sneak out to the garden. The first time in a couple of years. It's like she was on a very determined mission."

"What happened, exactly?"

"She gets extremely agitated," Eva paused. "Confused, rambling on about fixing the garden, crying about how she needs to leave and go home before the water finds her. One of the attendants found her kneeling in the muddy garden, digging frantically. She'd... soiled herself. She wasn't injured—but terrified, dirty, and rather frantic. We had to sedate her, and it's been a long time since that's happened. She's been rather withdrawn today, mainly sleeping. We're keeping her in her room for now, though."

Before the water found her lingered in my mind. What could Aunt Clara mean? And why was she so obsessed with a perfect garden? It seemed strange that my mother had also been obsessed with tending to her garden.

"So she's okay... physically though?"

"Yes." Eva nodded. "She's very fragile. Barely speaking today. We don't want to introduce any new stimulation—and I know you've come to deliver terrible news, and that is probably going to be a tough blow for Clara. We need her to be stabilized again beforehand."

I stared down at my hands, the old nail polish peeling in small flakes. I brushed one off and swallowed the disappointment of not having a visit today. Even though my aunt wouldn't be herself, I had needed the reassurance of a warm embrace.

"Could I stop by her door real quick? I wouldn't need to go in, or even say anything?" I met Eva's eyes, but I read the answer on her face before she provided it.

"Not today, I'm so sorry. She doesn't seem to recognize even familiar staff right now."

Hearing that, my disappointment suddenly seemed overly childish.

"Why don't you give us a call in a few days and we will see how she's doing then?" Nurse Eva stood, and I followed suit.

My mind drifted to the garden—imagining the rain falling, Aunt Clara's bare feet pressing into the wet soil, her arms raised against an invisible memory. She had always loved rain when I was a child. I could still picture her standing by the kitchen window during summer storms, humming softly while the thunder rolled in. She'd call me "Gracie-cloud," ruffle my hair, and tell me the rain washed away what the world didn't need anymore.

It was odd the rain had triggered her yesterday—and also for me. I'd thought it was the stress of being at the site where my father had driven into the lake, but maybe it was more than that—attached to the rain. It was too coincidental.

I left White Oak, feeling more like I'd been an intruder rather than a visitor. I'd left with more questions than answers. Stepping back outside, the chilly air hit me. I glanced up at the sky and hurried to my car, rushing home before the skies opened up.

When I got back home, the house seemed so empty—like it was waiting for me. Dust particles drifted in the slanted beam of light from the kitchen window, the air faintly cool and still. I didn't bother turning on the lights. I knew where I was going. My steps echoed softly down the hallway, past the knick-nack shelf and to my mother's bedroom door. Opening the door, I glanced down at the floor in front of the vanity.

There, still sitting open, was the box.

It was even bigger than I remembered—the letters and journals overflowing like the lid was never able to close. My eyes swam with my mother's handwriting. I sank down onto the floor and sat cross-legged, my hand resting on the edge of the box.

That same smell hit me again—papery, with a hint of lilacs. I let my fingers flip through the edges of card envelopes. Pulling out a smaller bundle, I immediately recognized the handwriting. Aunt Clara's. My mother's name, written across the front of the top envelope, with its familiar loops and curves.

The first card was simple—a watercolor of violets and the words *Thinking of You* across the front. I shifted into the small beam of light from the window before opening the card. Inside, Aunt Clara had written:

"Heidi-ho,

This morning when I woke up, I knew exactly what we needed, so I made your lemon cake recipe today. It reminded me of summers when we thought the world was ours to change. I hope this cake takes the sting out of everything else. Mama always said, when life hands you lemons, make lemon cake.

Love,

Clara."

The next card was for a birthday, based on the front, but the note inside was more vague and somber.

"You've always been the brave one, Heidi. Don't let anyone tell you otherwise. Don't let anyone make you feel small. I miss our long talks. No matter how lost you are, I will always come find you.

XO, Clara"

The words blurred as I read them. My eyes burned unexpectedly. I remembered what Dotty said about the two of them arguing, voices carrying all the way over to the next door. How did they go from these notes, which my mother had lovingly saved—to fighting, and eventually Clara having to live in a nursing home? Why couldn't she have lived with Mom?

I pressed the stack of those cards to my chest, aching inside for both of them, and all the things they'd never be able to say to each other again.

Setting those cards aside, I reached deeper into the box. Hoping for cheerful, funny, anything. Maybe old artwork of mine. A grocery list, to distract me. Anything.

I pulled out an envelope that didn't look like it belonged with the others. It was worn the way only an envelope opened over and over would be. Slipping out the letter, I could tell it had been folded and unfolded repeatedly until the creases were so worn in, it was nearly torn.

The handwriting gave me pause. It wasn't my mother's —nor Aunt Clara's. It was bold and slanted, more like a man's handwriting. Flipping the envelope back over, it simply said *Heidi* on the front.

My breath caught in my throat, and I hesitated, my thumb running over the letters. This letter felt intimate. The ink had splotches, what looked like droplets of water, possibly teardrops. In those spots, the ink had bled into little circles.

My eyes scanned the first couple of lines and my pulse

quickened. The roar of my heartbeat filled my ears, and the smell of lilacs—faintly on the papers before now seemed to fill my nostrils, building in the room until my head was swirling.

The words twisted as my eyes struggled to focus. The room tilted slightly. The smell was overwhelming now, thick and heady, as though the flowers were crowding in through the walls. I dropped the letter onto my lap, trying to steady myself, but the edges of the room had already begun to dissolve into darkness.

My lovely Heidi,

Something overcame me today, and the urge to put down into words my feelings for you became so strong, I found I had no other choice.

Meeting you has been one of the best things to ever happen in my life.

After Sylvia, I thought I'd never find love with another.

I know our situation isn't ideal. Hell, less than ideal. I recognize you're in a delicate situation. But all in due time, we will find our way. I refuse to dwell on the difficult parts, or the parts other people would find ugly.

For me, there can be nothing ugly about our love for one another.

Your situation is so unfair– and I know the difficulty and heartache it brings you. Should you ever find yourself in a position to leave, you risk leaving your daughter vulnerable to the hands of a monster. And for staying, I could never fault you.

But enough about that– I really wanted to write this today to let you know that I wake up in the mornings now with a smile on my lips because of you. The joy you have brought to my life is unmatched.

The moment I see you, my pulse speeds up, my hands get sweaty and I feel every bit of emotion and physical reaction as I would if I were a 15 year old boy experiencing love for the first time.

I want you to know you have made my life one thousand times better than I ever thought it could be– and that's here in our dire situation.

I long for the day I can fall asleep next to you and wake with your body pressed against mine.

With every fiber of my very being, I love you. –P.

CHAPTER ELEVEN

FAINTLY, *I hear it—the sound of water. A lap. A ripple. I can't tell if I'm in the water or just near it. The air smells like dirt, with a faint tang of fish.*

I have the feeling that I should run—I need to escape, but I don't understand why. There's a heaviness in my chest—a sense of doom.

Headlights flash, blinding me temporarily. My father's truck. Dented bumper, ugly air freshener swinging from the rearview mirror. It's already halfway engulfed in the water, tilted up as if trying to get one last glimpse of the moon. The lake is swallowing it, inch by inch.

The headlights flicker as the truck goes under with a GULP, bubbles rising up around it.

A door slams, and there he is again—my father. I turn back to the lake, but there's no sign of his truck. Was that real?

My father is stalking toward me through the shadows, his face taut with anger.

"What are you doing?" I call, my voice shaking.

But he doesn't answer. He keeps walking, eyes fixed on me. Not blinking. I shiver, wrapping my arms around myself.

He stops a couple of feet in front of me. His face dissolves, the anger now mixed with disappointment and sorrow. He opens his mouth, and water pours out. Then suddenly it's pouring out of his nose and ears and eyes too. It sprays out violently, like the lake is inside of him, exploding to get out.

I stumble backwards, my heel catching on a root. I trip, landing hard, the shock of cold mud slapping against my thighs, wetness soaking through my clothes. The air smells stronger—like rot.

Suddenly, I'm in the truck, buckled in and fighting to get the seatbelt loose. The water is rising in the truck as the lake swallows it, and I frantically tug at the seat belt. Why won't it unclip?

"Help me!" I scream. My voice echoes in the silence of the lake, coming back to me, jagged and warped. The water climbs higher, reaching my chin and I tip my head back, gasping for air. Soon, the water will overcome me. My lungs seize as the pressure from the water makes it harder to take in gulps of air.

Then, before the water takes over me, my mother is suddenly there. A giant, standing in the water, reaching down with long arms to lift the truck out of the water, letting it dangle between her fingers. Setting it down gently on the shore and opening the door as I tear free from the seat belt. She reaches in with her giant hand and lifts me out, resting me on her shoulder, gently patting my back.

"There, there, Grace. It's okay. It's all over." Her words envelope me in warmth.

I woke up gasping. The blackout dissolved in layers—first the smell of lilacs faded, the spinning of the room slowed, and the buzzing in my head slowly quieted to nothing. My shirt clung to my chest—soaked. For a moment, I was confused, thinking it hadn't been a dream, but I realized then it's sweat. Just sweat. I exhaled.

My heart was hammering away in my chest. The room was dimmer than it had been, and I realized I'd been out for at least a few hours. I sat up, and the letter fell from my lap.

The letter was more intimate than I ever thought anyone would even speak to my mother. I picked it up, letting my eyes scan those words again, burning into my retinas until I'd be able to picture that letter anytime, anywhere. Just enough to torture myself with.

I massaged my temples, trying to settle the throbbing. The dream felt too real to be a dream. It felt like a message. Maybe my mother had spent her whole life protecting me from my father.

Standing, I headed out to the kitchen and downed an entire glass of ice water before refilling it. I shrugged out of my damp shirt and pulled on a sweatshirt I'd left on the couch. Sinking into the cushions, I closed my eyes.

The dream replayed itself behind my eyelids, sharper this time. My father's silence, the way the water rose to my chin. The panic. The water poured out of my father, adding to the level drowning me. The way he stared at me while I was scared and struggling.

And my mother swooping in—so big and powerful, almost out of nowhere. Saving me. It felt so literal. Always saving me.

The last time I saw my father alive, he'd been sitting on the porch, a half-empty bottle at his feet, the night heavy around him. He'd looked up as I left, eyes glassy, and mumbled, "You think you know everything. Your mother ain't no saint."

I'd ignored him, brushing it off as a drunken rant. I

wanted to go hang out with Vanessa—we hadn't seen each other since leaving for our separate colleges, and I wanted to catch up with her. So I hadn't stopped to wonder what my father could mean.

The wind shifted outside, brushing against the house like a hand testing the walls. Down the hall, something creaked. I told myself it was the boards contracting with the cold, but I couldn't shake the feeling that the dream was still moving through the room with me, invisible but watching. A shiver ran through me that I tried to shake off.

I glanced at the window. My reflection stared back—pale face, dark eyes, hair sticking to my forehead. For a moment, I thought I saw someone else behind me, but when I turned, the space was empty.

I couldn't get rid of this feeling of a presence there—of being watched. Angling myself so I could lie back without my back to the room, I set my glass on the coffee table. I thought about the lake, my mind swirling.

Confusion took over as I tried to make sense of everything. The letter I'd read insinuated my mother was protecting me from my father—but my dad had said she was no saint either. And… maybe that was true. After all, who wrote her this love letter? Did my father drive into the lake on purpose, after realizing my mother was … cheating on him?

A jolt rolled through me, forcing me to accept the truth. The letter I found meant my mother had an affair.

I'd always assumed my father driving into the lake had been nothing but a drunken accident. But maybe it was more. Maybe that's what he was trying to tell me. What if he had found out about this letter from "P." and couldn't bear it?

I didn't go back to sleep that night. Dawn rolled in around me, as I curled up in the afghan on the couch, eyes burning and dry from exhaustion. The first gray light crept across the floorboards, revealing the dust on the furniture, the cracks in the paint. I sat there watching it until I could almost believe the night never happened.

By the time the sun rose, beams dancing across the floor, I'd convinced myself the dream was merely a dream. My imagination got away from me.

I got up and went to the bathroom where I splashed cold water on my face until it burned. My body moved with a stiffness, as though I'd aged ten years overnight.

Maybe my mother lived with a secret for decades—trapped between two men, one who wanted to save her and one who refused to let her go. Maybe she thought silence was the safest choice. Maybe she thought if I never knew, it would never matter.

CHAPTER TWELVE

WHEN THE INTERNET company called the next morning to tell me they needed to reschedule my hookup, I let work know I was going to be out a little longer than I originally thought. My boss was accommodating and told me not to worry about any of my cases. So I tried to force myself not to check work emails, as I could see they were being handled, and double checking behind people would be rude.

After a quick appointment to meet the attorney, I had the paperwork for the house—and power of attorney over my Aunt Clara. I'd been shocked the house was completely paid off and the attorney had handed me a large check made out to me. He said there was another bank account still in probate—I'd get the rest of that money too, once any creditors were paid off. There didn't seem to be many.

Without work to distract me, I had nothing else to do other than clean up my mother's house, or, as the paperwork declared, my house now. I decided to try to tackle the front yard, which was overgrown with weeds and bushes. She must have all the tools for it since the backyard was pristine.

Dragging everything out, I got busy trimming, pulling, and cleaning everything up. Multiple bags of leaves, weeds, and bush trimmings later, I was satisfied the front yard was up to par. A quick survey of the porch and roof told me I needed to get those things fixed as well.

Remembering Dotty's casserole dish, I went inside and washed up quickly before grabbing the dish and heading next door. If anyone could recommend a handyman, it would be the Paulsons.

"Well hello, Grace, what a pleasant surprise!" Dotty said as she opened the door. "How did you like the chicken and rice dish?" she asked, waving me inside.

"Oh, it was delicious. This is exactly what I needed—thank you so much! Here's your dish." I held it out awkwardly. She smiled and carried it into the kitchen. I assumed I was meant to follow, as she was chattering away, so I did. I was surprised to see that their kitchen had been updated. Somehow I'd expected them to still have the same ugly counters and cabinets my mother's house had—the original ones installed by the builders. But a glossy granite countertop and bright white cabinets made her kitchen modern. I glanced down at the tiles. No stains or aging.

"Your home is very nice," I commented and Dotty smiled.

"Thank you! Can I grab you a pop? I don't drink them myself anymore, but we still keep the fridge stocked for my daughter and grandkids when they come." I shook my head as my mind tried to reconcile Dotty having a kid of her own. I'd forgotten about her daughter because she was at least ten years older than me.

"Actually, I was wondering if you might know a handyman. There's a few things I need done around the house that I can't do myself."

"Oh yes, I'm sure we do. Ralph!" Dotty shouting to her husband startled me. I'd never heard her raise her voice before. Ralph shuffled in and nodded to me in way of a greeting.

"Hello Mr. Paulson. You look well."

"Thank you, you're Heidi's girl, aren't you?" When I nodded, he smiled and nodded back. "Nice lady, she was. Sorry to hear what happened." His gruff voice was comforting.

"Thank you. That means a lot. I hope it's not a bother, but I was hoping you might know a handyman I could call to do some work around the house?"

"Oh yes, of course, let me get you my guy's number. Good guy—does a lot of odd jobs. His name is Henry." Ralph paused as he flipped through the little papers stuck on the fridge and pulled out a sticky note. Dotty grabbed a pen and piece of paper and copied the name and number down for me. "This guy is decent too." Ralph handed me a business card. *Hall It Away*. The name underneath, I assumed was the owner: Graham Hall.

"Clever name." I tipped my chin to the card.

"Yeah, it sure is, and he's good at what he does. If you need to clear out any junk, it can be easier than loading it up to go donate it. You can take this card with you—we have a few hanging around."

"I really appreciate it. I'm going to go call both of these now. Thank you both so much." I stood and made my way toward the front door.

"So are you planning on selling the house, dear?" Dotty asked, following me, as Ralph wandered back to plop into his recliner in the living room. That room had also had some updates. Old beige carpeting, replaced with a beautiful hardwood floor. Modern furniture. Paint that hadn't faded with time.

"Well, I hadn't thought about it much—I mean this is all so sudden. I think, either way, it needs repairs. I could sell it, rent it or… I don't know…" I let my sentence fall off, having been about to say I could stay. The thought hadn't occurred to me before, but it didn't seem as outlandish as I would have thought a week ago.

"Oh, I see." Dotty wrung her hands together, her mouth opening and closing like a fish out of water.

"What is it?" I asked, because there was clearly more she wanted to say.

"Well… maybe it's selfish of me to mention, but I'd hate to deal with renters changing out all the time or… I guess I'd hoped you'd end up staying." She looked almost wistful. The woman barely knew me, why would it matter to her?

"I understand." I patted her arm. I didn't understand, but it seemed to make her feel better as she smiled brightly and told me goodbye, promising to bring me homemade muffins later in the week.

Back home, I sat down at the kitchen table and made the phone calls, scheduling work that needed to be done. Then I grabbed an empty box and went back out to the living room, determined to make decisions about the decor. Tossing in an ugly lamp and a set of strange beaded coasters, I thumbed through a few books on the shelf. Mostly inspirational, I pulled them out, flipping through each before adding it to the box.

I paused at the shelf of figurines. I didn't particularly want all of these, but could I sell them? Sighing, I began to move them all to one side of the shelf for now. I paused. The figurine with the broken neck was missing. I sorted back through the dolls, but she wasn't there. I checked on the floor around the shelf in case she'd fallen off—but nothing.

Turning back to the room, I did a quick inventory of everything else. And when my eyes landed on the fireplace mantel, there she was. I didn't remember ever moving the porcelain doll. Yet now she was perched neatly, her painted eyes seemingly glinting at me across the room.

A strange chill ran through me, the kind that wasn't cold but crawled along the spine anyway. The doll's placement felt deliberate. It was facing outward, carefully displayed, as if it had been waiting to be seen.

I took a step closer, the wood floor creaking under my feet. That's when I saw it—the urn. It sat beside the doll, dark and gleaming in the low light. My father's initials were engraved on the front, and beneath them, two crossed hockey sticks. I froze.

I'd never seen it before. I had never even thought about Mom keeping his ashes. I was surprised she chose this decorative urn. Sentimentality was never her way with my dad, at least not in my memory. But there they were—the hockey sticks—etched with such care it almost hurt to look at them.

Dad used to talk about hockey all the time when I was still little, though never without a shadow crossing his face. After what happened to his brother, a freak accident, but he'd never skated again. It made me think for a moment—no wonder he eventually was led down the path to drinking. And no wonder he'd ultimately left this earth to the same lake that had taken his brother.

I'd never seen my father's eyes twinkle the way they had when he talked about his big brother. The adoration was evident. For the first time in my life, I considered what a traumatic event my dad had been through when he was so young.

Now, staring at the doll and the urn side by side, I couldn't shake the feeling that something—or *someone*—had arranged them precisely so.

BLEEDING HEARTS CHRONICLE

Tragic Ice Accident Claims Life of Local Teen

December 2, 1969 – Bleeding Hearts Valley

What began as a weekend afternoon of outdoor fun ended in heartbreak Saturday when a 15-year-old boy lost his life after falling through thin ice on Moon Lake.

According to local authorities, two brothers—ages 15 and 12—had gone out to play ice hockey on the frozen lake around 3 p.m. Witnesses say the boys had been skating too far from the shore when the ice suddenly gave way.

"The younger brother managed to crawl back to solid ice and call for help, but his older brother went under before anyone could reach him," said Fire Chief Robert Tradwell during a press briefing Sunday morning.

Emergency crews arrived within minutes, but rescue efforts were hindered by frigid water and unstable ice conditions. Divers recovered the teen's body approximately 55 minutes later.

Officials described the ice as being less than two inches thick in some areas—far below the minimum safety recommendation of four inches for ice skating or recreation.

"This is every family's worst nightmare," said Sheriff Travis Gamble. "Our hearts go out to the parents and the younger brother who witnessed this tragedy."

Neighbors have placed flowers, hockey sticks, and candles near the lakes' edge in memory of the victim, described by friends as a "kind, athletic kid who loved the game and always looked out for his little brother."

Authorities are urging residents to use caution as temperatures fluctuate and local lakes and ponds begin to freeze. "No ice is ever completely safe," Chief Robert warned. "Please check the thickness before stepping out and never go alone."

A vigil is planned for Tuesday evening at BHV High School.

CHAPTER THIRTEEN

I WOKE UP WITH A START, the echo of footsteps still fading in my mind. For a moment, I wasn't sure if I was awake or still trapped in the same dream—haunting me for nights. The house was dark and heavy with silence, it made every creak in the floorboards sound like a whisper. I sat up, the sheets twisted around my legs, heart pounding as I tried to shake off the image of shadowy figures moving through the hallway. The air was colder than usual, and for the briefest moment, I thought I saw something shift near the doorway. But when I blinked, it was gone.

The dream had left me uneasy, more than it should have. Maybe it was because of everything I'd been uncovering lately—the letters and cards, my father's urn, and the doll moving all by itself. Whatever it was, I couldn't ignore it anymore. The house felt alive with secrets, and the walls seemed to hold their breath every time I asked the wrong question.

I thought about my mother's box again. I padded down the stairs, still in my nightshirt, and entered her bedroom. This time I pulled the box up on the bed with me. I hesitated, fingers tracing the edge of a journal. What else might I find? How many more secrets had my mother buried? But I couldn't turn away now. The urge to know everything was burning inside, a little flame growing bigger and bigger. I needed answers.

I lifted a smaller journal out, a beautiful lilac leather bound book. Opening it, my eyes flicked to the date. 1998.

Pat and I had another argument. Grace is about to turn six and I'd desperately like to give her a sibling before she's much older, but he can't seem to wrap his head around it. I've noticed whenever it comes up, he drinks more than usual. He's been drinking a lot lately.

After our argument, I found him on the porch, and I could tell he'd been crying. I think his reluctance to have a second child must have to do with losing his brother. I don't know why, but I guess the thought of Grace having a sibling is triggering unresolved issues. I tried to suggest he see a counselor but it made him more angry.

I'm feeling heartbroken over it—because my life would be so much lonelier without my sister. I want Grace to have that. I don't know what to do anymore.

I ran my thumb over the impression of the words where my mother must have been pressing down hard with the pen.

Flipping through the rest of that journal, it became clear her longing for another baby came from a deeply emotional and hopeful place. She seemed to have envisioned a fuller family, believing another child would bring new joy, and make my life better. My dad's reluctance continued to cast a shadow over her hopes. The emotion on the pages was evident—splotched ink, hard pressed indents, clearly my mother had experienced a range of emotions over this. It was clear she had loved both me and my father deeply.

This journal seemed to be a descent into a darkness for my father, and a great divide in their marriage. The entries alternated between her empathy for my father and full fledged anger at his inability to compromise or even discuss it fully. My mother's frustration and hopelessness built with every entry.

I couldn't stop reading once I started, and the entries went from mentioning arguments about having another baby to more types of arguments—about me, my father's drinking, his withdrawal.

My heart broke for her with every entry—I could feel the pain emanating from the pages. I'd never known any of this, but I saw this must have been when things soured for my parents. And when my father had gradually drifted away from both of us.

The entries spanned two years, sporadic with no real pattern or routine of when she wrote. It was clearly after big arguments. I flipped to the final entry.

I feel like I'm at the end of the rope here. Pat's drinking has gotten worse—it's really bad now. I can't believe the fights we've had. Grace hides in her bedroom when he starts yelling. It's getting scary.

Most of the time, I try to avoid setting him off. I stopped mentioning the entire subject of having a baby months ago, but it doesn't seem to have mattered. The space between us has continued to grow and grow.

The fights are getting more frequent. Last week Pat threw the remote across the room, shattering one of my porcelain figurines. He apologized profusely—I think it shocked him more than me.

But then last night… well I can't believe I am even writing these words down in ink. I don't know what to do. I can't talk to anyone about this. But I need to get it out.

Last night, Pat was drunker than I've ever seen him. He was screaming at me, ranting about who knows what. Grace was so scared she ran up to her room, and for that I'm glad, because Pat hit me. It was only the one time, and I could tell he felt so bad after. The look in his eyes. BUT HE HIT ME! I still cannot believe it. I'm going to have to figure out how to use cover up to cover the bruise on my cheek before I go back to work Monday.

After it was over, he charged out of the house. I was so afraid he was going to get in his truck and drive off, but when I looked out the front window, he was passed out in the driver's seat.

I iced my cheek and did my best to pull my hair forward to cover the bruise before I went upstairs to find Grace. She was hiding in her closet, clutching a teddy bear to her chest. I felt so bad.

For the first time, I'm so glad we decided not to have another baby. I mean, we didn't ever decide, Pat refused. But I'm glad it hasn't happened. How could I protect two kids from this mess when I can't even keep Gracie from it?

CHAPTER FOURTEEN

A LOUD KNOCK at the front door interrupted me from reading further. My hand froze over the page. I stared at the words until they blurred, hoping whoever it was would go away. The second knock came faster. Three sharp raps rattled the glass in the front door. I closed the journal gently, feeling the imprint of the letters against my fingertips one more time. The afternoon light had dimmed without me noticing. I couldn't believe how much time must have passed.

The third knock came, more insistent, as if they knew I was inside debating whether to answer. Sighing, I smoothed my shirt down and made my way to the door.

When I opened the door, the realtor, Thomas, was facing outwards and did a quick swivel, pasting on a huge smile. It was like catching a glimpse of a cheesy toothpaste commercial, if only there had been a fake twinkle over a tooth.

"Hello, Ms. Jenkins! You *are* home. I assumed since your car was—but I was about to give up…" He shrugged, and I had to bite my tongue to avoid telling him I wished he had. "Sorry to drop by unannounced again, but I was in the neighborhood and thought I'd check in."

"Check in?" I leaned against the door frame, arms crossed.

"Right, to see if you'd thought things through more—changed your mind at all…"

"No, I haven't." There was a bite to my voice I hadn't intended, but the guy gave me the creeps. I couldn't identify why, but something about him seemed off.

"Right, right." Thomas nodded, hands raised in mock surrender. The exaggerated look on his face made me want to slam the door in it. "And I completely respect that. But I have to tell you, to be frankly honest, well—opportunities like this don't happen often. The market's in a strange place right now. You'd be surprised what people would be willing to pay."

"Oh, I'm sure I would, but I'm still not interested."

"So… are you staying?" His voice sounded different all the sudden, more personal—almost a mix of surprise and horror. "Moving back to town? Going to live in this whole house all by yourself?" The way he said it sounded almost… threatening.

"I love this house. And my neighbors are great. They keep a close watch. I love the quiet here." At least that much was true.

"Quiet is nice." His gaze flicked over my shoulder into the house behind me. I wondered what he was trying to see. "Until it isn't. That's what I tried to tell your… " He stopped mid-sentence like he thought better of it.

For a minute, neither of us spoke. The only sound was the creak of the rotting porch boards under his weight and the faint hum of the refrigerator from the kitchen.

Then, as if catching himself, he laughed—a quick, too-bright forced sound. "Oh, that sounded ominous, didn't it? Sorry, didn't mean to spook you. I meant places like this can get lonely. Young and single—you should be in a trendy condo in a bigger city."

"I'm fine here." I found myself saying. And the truth in it surprised me. I didn't miss the city one bit.

"Of course." He nodded slowly, eyes still roaming past me, studying the fireplace like he was memorizing it. "You know, folks think these old houses have… character. But character is expensive to maintain, isn't it?"

"Did you come here to try to bully me into selling, Thomas?"

He blinked, then smiled. It almost seemed genuine this time. "Touché, Grace. You've got spirit. I like that." There with the use of my first name again. I was taken aback, but I couldn't tell if it was intentional or not. Did he want me to know he had done his research? Or was it an unintentional slip-up?

He rocked back on his heels, the silence hanging between us. "Well," he said finally, "I didn't mean to take up your evening. I wanted to remind you I'm around if you change your mind."

"I'm not going to." I exhaled with frustration. Why couldn't this guy take a hint?

"Hey," he said, "I didn't mean to come across pushy. I get the sense you've been keeping to yourself out here. A neighborhood like this can make you forget there's a world beyond these streets."

"Maybe that's the point," I countered.

He chuckled. "Fair enough. But you know, there's a great little coffee shop in town—Bleeding Brews? Best coffee around. Maybe you'd let me buy you a cup. Talk about anything *but* real estate." I didn't tell him, but I was familiar with Bleeding Brews. I wasn't surprised to hear they were still open either. It was a great little coffee shop. I was surprised that a jerk like Thomas went there.

"I don't think I..."

"Just coffee," he interrupted. "Friendly company. New in town, I'm sure you could use a friend." I didn't contradict him. If he knew this was my mother's house, why was he assuming I was new in town? "Maybe more than a friend," he added, the corner of his mouth lifting. Bile burned the back of my throat. This guy was a walking red flag.

I forced a laugh. "I'll think about it." This kind of guy wouldn't take rejection lightly, and at this point, I wanted him off my porch. "I'll call you if the answer is yes," I told him.

For a long moment, Thomas didn't move. His gaze lingered, tracing over my face, my shoulder, then drifting again toward the dim interior behind me. Finally, he exhaled and stepped back.

"Okay." He nodded. "Well, you take care then. Hope to hear from you soon."

I stood in the doorway, watching him head back to his vehicle. I waited until he was backing out of the driveway and I could no longer see him driving down the street. Then I went back inside and closed the door. Locking the knob, I reached up, hand trembling, and locked the deadbolt as well.

I had errands to run, but they could wait another day. I decided to fix myself a sandwich to eat while I finished reading the last journal entry.

CHAPTER FIFTEEN

THE GRAVEL CRUNCHED under my tires as I pulled into the driveway after running my errands, the afternoon sun slanting low and gold. I turned off the engine, staring in my rearview mirror at the truck parked in front of the house. I recognized it immediately. Thomas. But he wasn't in the driver seat.

But then I noticed him. He hadn't noticed me yet.

There he was, rounding the corner of the house, clipboard in hand, tape measure scrolled out. He had clearly been wandering around the property. I watched as he scratched down a note on his papers. No doubt, measurements.

He was wearing the same ugly suit from the last time I saw him, the one that seemed a size too tight around the shoulders. His hair was slicked down flat, smirking to himself like he had found a suitcase full of hundred dollar bills.

I opened my door slowly. "Thomas?"

He jerked up, confirming he hadn't heard my car pull

in. His smile appeared instantly, sharp and bright. "Oh! Hey there. You startled me."

"I startled *you?*" He had the balls to say, sneaking around *my* property. Wow, the audacity. I got out, closing the door harder than I needed to. "What are you doing here?"

"Oh, just... you know." He held up the clipboard, like it explained everything. "Taking notes in case you change your mind."

His nonchalance, the sense of entitlement shifted something in me. As leery as I had felt before, I could feel anger burn up inside my chest, grasping at my throat. It was almost dizzying how quickly I felt anger. It surpassed the slight irritation I should have felt.

"How dare you?" I seethed. My blood boiled.

He blinked. "Right, of course. Of course. I—well, I was in the neighborhood and figured in case you'd thought more about…"

"You sure do seem to be 'in the neighborhood' a lot, Thomas. What business do you have around here anyway?"

His smile twitched at the corner. "Oh, you know, I handle a lot of listings around here."

"Uh-huh." I folded my arms. "Thomas, I don't like people showing up on my property without asking. Especially not people who I've already clearly declined, and they should've moved on."

He took a small step back, the toe of his polished shoe catching on a bit of gravel. "I totally understand. I didn't mean to intrude. It was merely professional curiosity—and yeah, a little hopeful?" His attempt at a sheepish look fell flat.

"Professional curiosity can get you arrested for trespassing," I said, voice low. "You know that, right? Maybe I should call the police now, make it official."

That did it—the smile faltered completely. His eyes darted toward the street, then back to me, calculating. "Now, there's no need for threats," he said quickly, holding up both hands. "I was about to leave anyway."

"Not before you tell me what you're really doing here."

"Nothing! I swear, nothing." But 'nothing' didn't include a clipboard and tape measure.

"You've been sniffing around since the day I arrived, I suspect. You show up unannounced, pretend you're checking things, you keep asking about selling—pushing —" I stopped myself, narrowing my eyes. "I know realtors want to make a commission, but let's face it—this is too much. I'm sure you've been told no before? What is it you're looking for, Thomas?"

He opened his mouth, then closed it. The clipboard shifted in his hands. For a split second, I saw panic flicker across his face. Then, in his hurry to retreat, he fumbled and the clipboard slipped. Papers spilled out, and the breeze caught them, sending them fluttering across the yard.

"Oh, damn it," he muttered, dropping to his knees to grab them. His movements were clumsy now, desperate. He clutched at one, then another, stuffing them back into the folder without even looking. One sheet tumbled behind the bush by the front porch, vanishing from sight. He didn't notice.

"Thomas," I said sharply. "What's this about? Why are you so jumpy?"

He stood, clutching the messy pile of papers to his chest like they might fall apart again. His eyes darted everywhere except at me. "It's nothing. Just old records, property forms, I—I should be going. My next appointment—"

"You're not fooling anyone." I stepped closer. "If you keep sneaking around, I'll file a restraining order. You understand? Whatever you want, you're not getting it."

Something flickered behind his eyes then—not fear exactly, but close to it. Guilt or maybe regret? He looked like he'd realized he'd been caught one step too soon.

"I think there's been a misunderstanding," he said, his voice too calm now. "But I hear you. Loud and clear."

"Good," I warned. "Because next time, I won't be this polite."

He nodded stiffly, trying to collect what was left of his composure. "Stubborn as your mother," he muttered. I didn't have a chance to ask him what he meant before he turned and walked down the driveway, fast but controlled, his shoes crunching against the gravel. When he reached his vehicle, he paused long enough to force one last, brittle smile. "Have a nice day."

What did he mean that I was as stubborn as my mother? How would he know? Had he approached her to sell the house as well?

I waited until he was ducking into his truck before I walked over to the front porch and swiftly bent down, scooping up the paper. I tucked it against me before slipping into the house. Leaning against the door, I examined it.

City of Bleeding Hearts Valley
Department of Building & Safety
BUILDING PERMIT APPLICATION

PROJECT INFORMATION

Project Address: 518 Monmouth Drive, Bleeding Hearts Valley
Parcel Number: 763-48-8489
Zoning District: R-3 (Multifamily Residential)
Type of Work: Demolition of existing home and new construction of 5-story apartment complex (40 units)

OWNER / APPLICANT / CONTRACTOR

Property Owner: Thomas Andrews
Address: 518 Monmouth Drive, Bleeding Hearts Valley
Applicant/ Contractor: Skyview Builders, Inc. Contractor License No: EX-9876543
Contact: (555) 321-9876

PROJECT DESCRIPTION AND VALUATION

Total Building Area: 68,000 sq. ft.
Estimated Construction Cost: $8,500,000
Number of Stories: 5 Number of Units: 40
Building Height: Approximately 58 ft.

REQUIRED SUBMITTALS

- Site Plan (showing existing and proposed structures)
- Architectural Plans and Structural Calculations
- Energy Compliance Documents (Title 24)
- Soil Report (if required)
- Demolition Plan
- Waste Management Plan

ESTIMATED FEES (subject to review)

Plan Review Fee $7,500
Building Permit Fee $15,200
Impact Fees (Traffic, School, Park) $42,000
Demolition Fee $1,000

APPLICANT CERTIFICATION I hereby certify that I have read and examined this application and know the same to be true and correct.

Applicant Signature: _______________________ Date: ___________
Property Owner Signature: __________________ Date: ___________

CHAPTER SIXTEEN

I'D JUST FINISHED EXAMINING the paper when a loud commotion outside caught my attention. It sounded like people arguing. Peering out the window, Thomas's truck was still there, but he was no longer in it. I set the application down on the coffee table. Anger bubbled up in my chest. I had told this fool to leave. Why was he still here?

Opening the front door again, I was prepared to stomp out there and give him a piece of my mind, but the argument that had caught my attention heightened. I shifted my gaze to the other side of my property. Tucked behind the hedges that divided my lawn from the Paulsons', I could see two men standing next to a truck. Thomas was standing near them, his face contorted with… worry? Or maybe fear?

Both of the men were well over six feet tall, big burly men. One had his arms crossed, a flat look on his face, while the other was cracking his knuckles. They looked like a couple of stereotypical henchmen.

Slowly, I eased my door back until it was almost closed and then held my breath, focused on trying to hear what they were saying. Thomas' voice was hushed, but the other two clearly didn't care about being overheard.

"Listen jackass, you were told you had to have the money by last week. We gave you an extra week but you're out here pussy-footing around. What do you think you're going to gain, hanging around this beat-up property?" The knuckle-cracker was clearly the spokesman for the two intimidators. He gestured toward my house. He was asking what I basically wanted to know too. *Why was Thomas so interested in my house?*

"I told you—this is my next deal. Once I sell this property, I'll have this property set up in no time. I'll need a property manager and that's where we can shift things to Sam. He'll be getting the rent checks and can take his portion right off the top. Once the loan is paid, that's all I care about."

"I'm not looking to manage your property, asshole. And we don't do layaway. You screwed us over with your *investment* deal to begin with. We won't make that mistake again. I highly suggested you find a way to get the money you owe us. You have ten days. And it's only ten days because Sam's your cousin, and he said we couldn't come break both your legs today. Because if it was up to me..." The knuckle crack was audible even from where I was eavesdropping.

Thomas glanced nervously around.

"Alright, I'll figure it out," he mumbled and rushed back to his truck. He didn't even turn back to look at the house as he peeled off onto the street. The other truck engine roared as they sped off in the opposite direction.

What the hell was Thomas mixed up in? Something wasn't right about that guy.

I pushed the front door closed the last inch or two and locked it. The permit on the coffee table caught my eye again, and I mulled over how buying my house might fit in with the pressure from these goons. One thing was for sure—Thomas was not the guy he was pretending to be.

Slipping my cell phone out of my pocket, I realized I'd missed a return phone call from the nursing home. I'd left a message for the nurse to let me know if Aunt Clara could have visitors yet.

Hello Ms. Jenkins, this is Nurse Eva at White Oak Manor. I'm returning your call. Clara has made a little progress toward stabilizing but I'd like to give her a couple more days. I've never seen her take so long to get back to her usual self. She's recognizing staff again, but she's mostly sitting around staring into space lately, writing notes to herself in her journal. Let's give it a few more days, alright?

Frustrated, I deleted the message. I didn't want to cause my aunt any undue stress, but I wanted to see her. The waiting was sitting heavy on my chest, like a weight I needed to shove off. I needed to tell her about my mother. It didn't feel right that she still didn't even know what had happened. Incoherent or not, I had to believe her subconscious would know.

Suddenly, I knew I needed to get through all of my mother's letters and journals, until I learned more about Aunt Clara, my mother, and everything... My curiosity had turned to this desperation to find out exactly what other secrets my mother had and what had happened between her and Aunt Clara.

Back in my mother's bedroom, I dug around in the box, lifting each unread journal out. I flipped through a few until I found one where I saw my aunt's name multiple times. I'd start there.

OCTOBER 2, 2014

I thought Clara was coming to terms with... everything. For a while, it even seemed like she was beginning to find her footing again, or at least pretending well enough that I wanted to believe it. But things have been getting worse—just a little at first, but then all at once. She's been coming over constantly, at all hours, saying she can't sleep. Sometimes she just sits on the couch and stares out the window, as if she's waiting for something—or someone—that never comes. Other nights she can't sit still, pacing from room to room until dawn, muttering to herself or bursting into tears without warning.

It's frightening, the way exhaustion has taken hold of her. You can see it in her eyes: the red rims, the dark circles underneath, the tremble in her hands when she reaches for her coffee. When she does finally fall asleep—usually for only an hour or two—she tosses and turns, whimpering, crying out like she's trapped in an endless nightmare. I try waking her, but it never feels like she's really back when she opens her eyes. It's as if she's caught between worlds, haunted by what happened.

I've started noticing other things—how she forgets to eat, how she shows up in the same clothes for days at a time, how she avoids sunlight like it hurts her. Days blend into weeks, and weeks into months, and still she drifts—no routine, no purpose, no spark left in her. I try to remind her of the things she used to love, but she shakes her head, eyes distant. It's like she's forgotten who she used to be.

I keep thinking back to when we were younger, way before all of this happened. Clara was always the strong one, the one who kept everyone else together. She used to laugh so easily—real laughter, the kind that filled a room. It's strange how someone can fade, how the light can drain from a person so gradually you barely notice until it's almost gone. I see her now and I barely recognize her.

I don't know how to help her. I thought we were in this together. If I had ever known what it would do to her, I never would have called her that night. But I needed my sister. I need her now too. I'm so lonely. All we have is each other. Now I don't even have her. I wish there was someone she could talk to. Or someone that could help us.

The house feels different when she's here, so heavy. I've suppressed my own feelings. I've tried to move on because I feel like I did what I had to do. But she can't.

I've started to dread her visits, though I feel awful admitting it. Every time I hear her knock, my stomach twists with a mix of worry and guilt. I want to help her, but I'm running out of things to say, and part of me is afraid she might pull me under too.

Last night she came over around midnight, trembling and incoherent. Said she couldn't be alone. She stayed until dawn, sitting by the window, eyes fixed on something I couldn't see. When she finally left, the silence that followed felt almost unbearable. I keep thinking about the way she looked when she turned to go—so small, so tired, like she'd been carrying a load far too heavy, for far too long.

I'm getting worried about her. I keep telling myself it's only going to be a rough patch, and she'll find her way back eventually. But deep down, I'm not sure I believe that anymore. She's unraveling, and I don't know how to stop it.

CHAPTER SEVENTEEN

AFTER SPENDING the morning decluttering my mother's bathroom toiletries, I felt too weird using the rest of her shampoos and lotions. I curled up in bed with the journal I'd started. I flipped through the pages, my eyes catching on 'Clara' over and over. The entries were frequent but short.

10/5/14 - Clara forgot her own name this morning. She laughed about it, she said it tasted wrong in her mouth. I told her to rest. She didn't like that.

I paused there, frowning, because the way my mother described it—almost clinically—felt wrong. The idea of my aunt forgetting her name seemed impossible. She'd always been so bright, a real force to reckon with. Strong and smart, so witty, I'd always seen her as a superhero.

• • •

10/8/2014 - She's hearing things again. The same voice, she says. Not the one from before. A new one.

My mother didn't elaborate there. I kept reading, soaking in every single sentence. Every entry added to the growing weight in my chest—that feeling of doom, like the world was weighing me down. I couldn't imagine what my mother must have felt like seeing her sister deteriorate this way. Reading my mother's notes, I could feel how she went from hope and fear to this blank emptiness, a total void of hope.

The notes went on and on, threading their way through all of October and November. The ones in early December turned from my aunt losing her way to becoming violent.

12/14/14 - Well, last night the neighbors called the police. Clara got completely out of hand. It started with her usual ranting, and then she was throwing a full fledged fit. Screaming, shouting, frantically waving her arms at me. She started throwing things at me, and I was getting worried she would try to hurt me. We got away with a warning from the police, but I don't know if they'll be so understanding next time.

The handwriting began to get more erratic. Where the lines of writing were neat, straight and uniform before, the writing was more frantic—large and sloppy, slanted across the pages.

• • •

1/5/15 - Christmas was exhausting—sad and lonely despite Clara staying with me. She won't go home anymore, so I went over and packed up everything important. I've called around and we are going to put her townhome up for sale. Clara said she won't go back there, so there's nothing else to do about it now.

1/20/15 - Clara refused to eat for two days. She said all the food smelled spoiled. It was the same food I was eating, so there was nothing wrong with it.

2/1/15 - Well, we got a fast offer on the townhome and they're closing next week. I've tried to talk to Clara about this—she's getting forgetful and I'm worried I can't keep her safe anymore. She turns on the gas burner and forgets to turn it off, she leaves the bathtub running until it's overfull.

2/15/15 - Clara wanders around the garden barefoot in the freezing cold. I can't get her to stop. I'm worried she's going to get frostbite. I found her out there in the middle of the night.

I blinked, heart stuttering. *The garden.* What was it about my aunt and gardens? I closed the journal then, for a moment to steady my breath. The house was silent except for the clock ticking in the background.

When I reopened the journal, I thought I'd skipped a few pages, but I realized my mother hadn't written in over a month.

4/1/15 - Tomorrow we move Clara into White Oak Manor. It's a great, cozy nursing home. But I still hate that I feel like I'm sending her off to be their problem. I'm so thankful the attorney agreed to come to the house, we filled out everything we needed for the power of attorney. I'm worried she won't even be able to answer for herself in the near future. I don't even know if the Clara I know and love is still in there. Her eyes look so empty now. I can't believe it's come to this. I've lost everyone I ever loved. Patrick twice—once so long ago and again four years ago. Grace, my sweet sweet Gracie. Losing her was the hardest. I did what I needed to do though, for her to be safe, to live a happy life. I hope. Phillip. And now Clara. I don't know how I will ever make it through days like this.

The entry went on, but I couldn't read any longer. The tears were pouring down my cheeks now. It was like I was experiencing the loss of everything my mother had lost, as well as everything I had lost. I was as alone as she had been then.

WHITE OAK MANOR

Intake Report
Resident Name: Clara Miller
Date of Admission: 4/2/2015
Date of Birth: 5/2/1950
Room Number:103
Admitting Physician: David Murray, M.D.
Primary Nurse: Eva Burke, RN

Reason for Admission: Admitted from sister's home for long term care.
Primary diagnosis: Delirium. Secondary diagnosis: Psychosis.

Functional Status:
Mobility: Independent
Activities of Daily Living:
Eating: Needs assist
Bathing: Needs assist
Dressing: Needs assist
Toileting: Independent

Cognitive & Behavioral Status:
Orientation: Disoriented/ Memory Loss
Mood/Affect: Depressed
Behavioral Concerns: Wandering, Agitation

Nutrition:
Diet Order: Regular
Appetite: Poor
Swallowing Issues: No

Vital Signs (on admission)
Temp: 98.6
BO: 125/85
HR: 82 BPM

SOCIAL SUPPORT INFORMATION:
Next of Kin: Heidi Jenkins, Sister
Power of Attorney: Heidie Jenkins

Filed by: Eva Burke, RN
Date/Time of Report: 4/2/2015 2:45PM

CHAPTER EIGHTEEN

BY THE NEXT MORNING, I'd packed up most of the obvious things I wouldn't want to keep. I'd decided there wasn't enough to pay the Hall it Away guy, so I made a quick trip to drop off my donation boxes. I thought about what I could do to pass the time. I couldn't read any more journals. *Not today*. The previous day had emotionally drained me. Without the internet, I couldn't work. And they didn't want me coming to see Aunt Clara yet.

I decided what I needed was exercise. I'd been lying around rotting for a week now, and it was starting to drag me down.

Over the years, I'd developed a regular gym habit. I loved working out to burn off steam. But I definitely hadn't been active out in nature. I made a mild effort to look presentable—leggings without holes, and a soft, thin sweatshirt. Popping in my ear buds, I started my workout playlist and headed down my street. I was ready to make my way around my old neighborhood and see what had changed. Maybe I could clear my mind.

As I picked up my pace, the air felt different—lighter,

carrying the faint scent of pine and damp earth. The cracked sidewalks were still lined with overgrown grass, and I could almost see my younger self racing down them on a bike, the wind tugging at my shirt. The trees I used to climb had grown taller and fuller, their branches now arching overhead to form a green canopy that filtered the afternoon sun into soft, golden beams. Every corner seemed to hum with a quiet nostalgia, the kind that makes you slow down to take it all in.

I followed the familiar curve of the road toward the small park at the end of the block, where the old swing set still stood. Birds darted between the bare branches, their songs mingling with the whisper of the few remaining leaves in the breeze. For a moment, it was as though time had folded back on itself, and I was simply home again—rooted in the place that shaped me, surrounded by the quiet beauty I'd once taken for granted.

I hadn't thought I'd missed all this, but as I sank into the swing, I noticed the seat and chain had been recently replaced. Letting my legs lift, I leaned back into it and let myself fly, pumping my legs harder and harder. I stared up at the clouds, and let everything else I had been thinking about all week melt off me, like the icicles that hang from your roof at the end of winter, slowly dripping until they either break off or disappear altogether.

I didn't know how long I sat on the swing, letting myself think about nothing but the shape of the clouds, or the way the chill in the air burned my throat. But eventually my stomach let out a loud grumble. Glancing at the time on my phone, I realized I'd missed lunch and it was nearly dinner time. Hopping off the swing, I headed up the street back toward home.

Before I rounded the curve toward my house, I stopped

in front of another house, almost as familiar as my own. The soft blue siding and crisp white trim. The large porch swing where we had spent hours in the summer drinking lemonade and dreaming about our futures. I'd been so preoccupied with my mother and her house, and everything with my aunt I hadn't even let myself think about Vanessa.

Vanessa Reed had been my best friend since they moved onto this street when we were both four. Through high school, and the summer after. And we had started college, still sending each other messages every day. She was my best friend, until she wasn't. I stared up at the house, wondering if Vanessa's parents still lived here.

I didn't have to wonder long, because the front door suddenly swung open. "Grace? Gracie Jenkins?" And there was Mrs. Reed, short and round enough to be soft and give the best hugs. She came out the front door with her hands extended. I felt ridiculous lingering at the end of the road, but Mrs. Reed had already stepped forward, arms hovering uncertainly at her sides, her smile held open as if waiting for me to close the distance.

I half-jogged, half-walked up the drive, nearly tripping up the steps to the porch. She wrapped her arms around me, her perfume like a comforting cloud encasing us. "I heard about your mother, honey. I'm so sorry..." She looked up at me, catching my eye, and I quickly looked away. Her eyes were damp and she reached up and wiped away a tear. Mrs. Reed and my mother had never been close friends, but Vanessa and I had been in and out of each other's houses enough, so they'd had a mutual respect for one another. "I didn't realize you were back in town, or I'd have come by to see you." I waved off her apology.

"Vanny, come see who's here." Mrs. Reed called over her shoulder and I froze. I hadn't expected Vanessa to be here. Anxiety rose up through my body, my throat burning with it. What would we say to each other? Her mother clearly didn't know how badly things had ended. She probably assumed we'd grown apart going to separate colleges. Or maybe that's what Vanessa had told her.

Vanessa appeared in the doorway behind her mother, and my breath caught, words tangling before they ever reached my tongue.

"Hey Grace." Her voice, softer than ever, was like a gentle whisper in the wind. "I heard you were back in town, I didn't know if I should..." She slid her eyes to her mother who suddenly acted busy.

"I'll let you girls get caught up!" Mrs. Reed's exclamation rang a little too bright, snapping into the air like a practiced line she'd rehearsed once too often. She disappeared into the house, and Vanessa stepped out onto the porch, pulling the door closed behind her. She stuffed her hands into her jeans pockets and wandered over to the porch swing. With a tip of her chin, she indicated for me to sit with her. I shrugged to myself and followed her.

Sinking into their enormous cushioned porch swing next to her, I could almost believe we had never stopped talking. We were eighteen again, bare feet kicked up on each other's laps, talking excitedly about the college experiences we hoped to have. Promising to tell each other everything.

Today though, we both sat on opposite ends, legs dangling below us as we gently swayed.

"I'm sorry to hear about your mom." Vanessa finally broke the silence, and I nodded, looking down at my hands. "Listen, I... can't claim to know or understand what you were going through after your dad died, but I'm sorry if I said or did the wrong things, but I—" I held up my hand to stop her.

"If it's alright with you, I don't want to talk about that. I mean, I barely remember why we stopped talking. I didn't come here today looking for you. Just so you know. I was walking around the neighborhood and your mom popped her head out. I didn't know you'd be here. Do you… do you… Live here?" My voice cracked at the end, not wanting to ask a question that would embarrass her, but not sure how to ask.

She laughed. "No, I like to check on my parents whenever I can. I come over for dinner a couple times a week. I rent an apartment downtown, but actually—I'm engaged… so my fiancé and I will be moving in together once my lease ends." She smiled shyly.

"Oh, congrats! So exciting!" I aimed for excitement, but the words came out thin, their dull echo reaching my own ears. It wasn't that I wasn't happy for her, it was how her life was such a contrast to mine right now, and I couldn't help the hollow feeling.

"So you moved back here after college, then?" I tried to recover.

"Yeah, I started on at Bleeding Hearts Chronicle—as a little peon of course, but I've worked my way up to my own byline." She smiled proudly. I pulled my mouth into a smile that felt a little hollow. Journalism had been the plan once. Big papers, bigger cities. Now she was back, and I wondered how things had unfolded along the way.

Before I could ask anything else, Mrs. Reed stepped outside. "Dinner's about done. Grace, would you like to stay for dinner? I made a goulash. Daniel and I are eating in the living room so he can watch his show, so you girls can sit at the kitchen table and chat." It was weird hearing her refer to Vanessa's father as Daniel.

As much as I wanted to high-tail it out of there, my stomach grumbled again. I'd have given anything for a hot home-cooked meal. So I found myself nodding with a surprised Vanessa staring on. I wondered if she didn't want me to stay, but it was too late. Mrs. Reed was already ushering into the kitchen and making herself scarce after filling our bowls.

We'd stuffed ourselves until we couldn't take another bite and caught up on basic small talk—avoiding everything important—when Vanessa finally crossed her hands and looked at me, seriousness etched on her face.

"I feel weird mentioning this but I'm working on an article right now about the number of people suspected of disappearing into Moon Lake—the ones who've been found, and the ones who... haven't..." Vanessa looked at me pointedly. I nodded but I didn't say anything. How awful for the families whose loved ones were never found.

"I was hoping we could maybe talk about your dad. I know it's a lot to ask. I feel like a terrible person now that I've said it out loud but it would help my research."

I blinked, the words landing heavier than they should have. My stomach tightened, a sharp mix of surprise and disbelief flashing across my face before I could stop it. "My dad?" I echoed, a short, humorless breath slipping out. "That's... not exactly something you just *bring up* for research." I folded my arms, irritation creeping into my voice despite my effort to stay calm. "I get that you're curious, but that was abrupt." I wasn't sure how anything I knew about my dad's accident would help her article.

"I'm sorry. You're right, I wasn't thinking. But I'd still like for you to consider it. No matter what you decide, I'd love to see you again. How long are you planning on being in town?"

Vanessa's question should have been a simple one. But the truth was, I'd already forgotten what life in the city was like. I didn't know if returning was even an option now.

"I-I'm not sure. A little while at least. Maybe we could go grab a coffee tomorrow?" I offered.

"That would be great. Do you want to meet up at Bleeding Brews?" she asked. For a second, I wanted to say no. Thomas's pushiness had tainted the very name of the business. But no, I wasn't going to let this dirtbag ruin my opportunity to have an amazing cup of coffee. So we agreed on a time, and Mrs. Reed hugged me goodbye one more time before I headed out the door and back to my own house, a walk that felt as familiar as if I'd walked it yesterday.

CHAPTER NINETEEN

AS I TURNED into my own driveway, dusk had already started to pull its long gray fingers over the trees. The house sat there, quiet and still, exactly as I'd left it that morning—or so I thought. But then I noticed marks on the walkway.

Footprints.

A trail of dark, muddy impressions wound their way from the side of the house near the gate, to the backyard, to the front. They disappeared halfway down the driveway. Someone had clearly been in my backyard, tromping around in the muddy bits of garden. The prints were big.

My heart skipped a beat. At first, fear prickled at the hair on the back of my neck. Did I need to get a lock for my back gate? My fear suddenly slid into anger, as I realized the one person it was likely to have been.

Thomas.

He came onto my property like he owned it—and now that I knew how desperately he wanted that to be the case, it made me even less willing to consider it. He couldn't take a hint.

"Fucking unbelievable," I muttered. I carefully went up the front porch steps, thankful the handyman was coming to do repairs the next day. I slipped inside the house and kicked off my own shoes. I wandered around downstairs, making sure nothing looked out of place, double checking the backdoor was locked and the windows secure. I didn't think he'd been inside—there wasn't anything inside the house he wanted anyway.

A sharp knock at the door made me jump and I whipped around, hurrying to the front door. I paused. He wouldn't be returning right now, would he? Another knock came, lighter this time.

"Grace? Are you home?"

I let out a shaky breath, relieved to hear Dotty's voice on the other side of the door. I unlocked the knob and opened it.

Dotty stood on the porch, looking around, clutching her cardigan close around her neck. Her gray curls were a mess, her eyes framed with worry.

"Oh you're home. Thank goodness," she said. "I stopped by a little bit ago, and I was starting to get worried."

"What's wrong?" I asked, stepping aside so she could come in.

She hesitated for a second and then bustled in. "Well I don't want to scare you, dear, but I saw a man nosing around your backyard earlier."

My stomach clenched. "You did?"

"Oh yes." She nodded, quick and emphatic. "It was about two hours ago. I was at the sink, doing the dishes—the window there looks straight over your driveway. I saw a man pull up in a truck and get out." She lifted a hand, as if marking the moment. "He went right to your front door.

Knocked, I think. Then a minute later he was back at his truck."

Dotty frowned. "I thought that was it, but then he stopped. Just stood there for a second. And then he turned and went around the side of the house." She drew in a breath. "I couldn't see him anymore, so I moved to the back door. From there, the fence blocks most of the yard—but he was tall. I could see his head over it." Her voice lowered. "He was walking around back there. Not just passing through—roaming."

She paused, finally, to breathe.

"Here, why don't you sit down." I gestured to the couch and she sat down with a loud sigh.

"So did you notice anything else?" I asked gently, sitting down next to her.

"No, he didn't stay long—he left shortly after. Are you having work done back there?"

"No, I'm not. What did he look like?"

Dotty frowned, squinting as she tried to recall. "Well, like I said, he was tall. Had dark hair, slicked down. He was wearing a suit—it looked too small for him though."

"Thomas," I said without thinking about it.

"Thomas? You know this man?"

"He's a realtor. He's been sniffing around the property. Rather pushy, and thinks a developer would be interested." Dotty's eyes went round, and the way her face tightened made it seem as though she was already picturing the place next door buzzing with people, too loud and too close for comfort. "Don't worry, I told him I wasn't interested in selling. He can't seem to take a hint."

Dotty's brows pinched together. "He has no right to be stomping around your property, dear. None at all."

"I know, believe me, I know." I patted her arm.

"Maybe you should call the police," Dotty suggested. "Trespassing is trespassing."

"Maybe." But I wouldn't. I didn't want the police poking around my house either. The thought made something knot tight just under my ribs, an instinctive recoil I couldn't quite shake. I pictured uniforms at my door, slow footsteps through rooms they didn't belong in, questions asked a little too carefully. My fingers curled into my palm, and I pushed the feeling down, telling myself—without much conviction—that it was only a precaution.

My mother could always handle everything without calling the cops. I knew I could handle this myself, too.

"Well, think about it. And if I see him out here again, I'll tell him he needs to leave. Your mother was obsessed with keeping the back garden immaculate. I can't imagine she would want a busybody tramping around in her plants." Apparently hearing I didn't want him here was giving her a boost of courage. I chuckled.

"There's no need. If he keeps hanging around, I'll see about getting a restraining order," I said, and Dotty nodded vehemently.

"Okay dear, well I'm going to get back home. It's getting late." Dotty stood and I walked her to the door.

"Be careful of those steps, please. The handyman is coming tomorrow to fix them," I told her and she gripped the railing, nodding.

"Oh I am."

Standing on the porch, I crossed my arms across my chest, trying to warm myself in the chill of the evening. I waited until Dotty had walked across to her own porch. She opened her door and slipped in. I smiled to myself for a moment. My annoyance at having a little nosy old lady next door was diminishing. Dotty was growing on me.

I turned back into the house and locked the door behind me.

Despite finding the footsteps and the surprise of seeing Vanessa, my evening had turned out pretty well. The walk and dinner at the Reed's had lifted my mood. Even Dotty's little visit had warmed my heart. Feeling replenished, I decided to dive into another one of Mom's journals. Heading back into her room, I dug through the book, flipping open to see the date on the first entries. I wasn't sure what I was looking for until I found one dated April 2011. My senior year of high school. Before… everything.

APRIL 23, 2011

I can't believe my baby girl is going to be leaving in just a few short months. Even though I'm so proud of her for being accepted to her first college choice, I can't help but wish it wasn't 200 miles away. I know, 200 miles is nothing compared to a few of her classmates. Little Vanessa is going to a school in New York. NEW YORK! Thank god my Gracie isn't going that far. I don't know how Maggie will cope. But still... 200 miles will be the furthest away I've ever been from my girl.

I keep trying to imagine what the house will be like without her here, without her pop music trickling down the stairs. Without her book-bag dumped at the doorway. The house is going to feel so empty.

I know I'll need to stay busy—take a class or take up a new hobby. Maybe I'll learn how to do watercolor or I'll plant that garden I'm always claiming I'll get around to.

I'm not sure how things will go with it being Pat and me home alone all the time. I don't know if things will get worse or better. Left all alone, I can only hope he will mellow out, but I wonder if Grace being here is what has held him back from doing… worse.

I know I'm going to miss her so much. Those daily hugs!

On a totally different note—maybe I'll have more chances to see P. The guilt of seeing him has faded. I've been through so much, and even though I know it's all wrong, when I see him, it feels nothing but right.

CHAPTER TWENTY

ANOTHER RESTLESS NIGHT had me waking up jonesing for the strongest coffee I could get my hands on. My dreams had been filled with snippets of my mother running off with a man. I never saw his face, but I knew it was the "P." from the journal—the same one from the love letter. Laying in bed fantasizing about a giant cup of coffee, I somehow managed to drift back into a deep sleep. So deep that when I woke up hours later, I realized it was already almost time to meet Vanessa.

I forced myself into the shower. I couldn't believe I'd slept almost the entire day. Afterward, standing at the sink, I decided I should cover up the dark circles under my eyes. Despite catching up on sleep, they were still prominent. Digging through my makeup bag, I found my concealer—which I hadn't touched since I'd last gone into the office. The thought of putting it on my face made me cringe, but I couldn't go out that way.

A quick touch of makeup and a fuzzy sweater wrapped around me, and I was ready to go. The drive to the coffee shop was quick and I could have kissed the door as I swung it open.

Bleeding Brews looked almost exactly the same as it had when Vanessa and I used to sneak in after skipping last period senior year—same chalkboard menu with the messy lettering, same rust-colored brick walls, even the same old espresso machine still sounded like it might explode any second. The only change was the increased scattering of laptops open at every table, and a soft hum of conversation filling the air instead of teenage laughter. A shift in customer demographics.

I ordered my cup of coffee quickly and glanced around the café.

Vanessa waved me over from a corner booth. She'd already ordered—typical—and was stirring sugar into her coffee with the same slow, thoughtful motion I remembered.

"Hi," she said as I slid into the booth across from her. "I can't believe you actually came. I thought you might bail."

I smiled weakly. "I almost did. It's been a week of chaos."

She nodded. "I understand."

"The house has been… a whole presence itself. And I don't have the internet hooked up yet, so I feel like I'm living in the dark ages. My cell phone provider apparently had spotty service here too. Might need to switch… "

Vanessa lifted her eyebrows. "No WiFi? How are you even surviving?"

"I'm not. I can't stream anything, I can't work, I can't even Google how to fix the leaky faucet in the kitchen. I've been... staring at walls and pretending I remember how to read a book. I can't believe my mother didn't use the Internet!" It wasn't the whole truth, but I wasn't ready to tell Vanessa about the journals or letters.

She grinned, taking a sip. "At least it's not like my parents. You know they still think their router is haunted? My dad swears it only works when he stands in the hallway and holds his phone up like he's blessing it."

That made me laugh, really laugh, for the first time in days. "Maybe he's onto the solution. Maybe the WiFi gods demand devotion. I should try that with my cell phone!"

"Oh, he's devoted," she said, smiling. "Every Sunday morning ritual: unplug, plug back in, curse, repeat. It's practically a religion at this point."

For a moment, it was easy again. Just me and my best friend joking over coffee, slipping into the familiar rhythms that used to come so naturally. But then her eyes shifted, getting a particular sharpness I'd always known meant she was working up to a big ask.

"So." Vanessa leaned back against the booth. "I mentioned I wanted to write an article. About the people lost to the lake?"

The words dropped between us like a pebble into still water. My stomach tightened. She certainly wasted no time. Typical Vanessa—it was how I'd always known she'd make an amazing reporter. And why I was surprised she wasn't working for The New York Times or another big name paper.

"Yeah," I said, careful to keep my tone neutral. "You mentioned it."

She nodded slowly, gauging my reaction. "I've been doing research. There are a lot more stories than people realize. Suicides, accidents, disappearances—many never made the news."

The blood rushed to my ears. I could already tell where

this was going. I stared down at my cup, watching the faint swirl of cream still mixing into the coffee. "That sounds... heavy."

"It is," she admitted. "But it's important, you know? People forget how much the lake takes."

I forced a small nod, suddenly very aware of the hum of the espresso machine and the laughter from the next table over.

She hesitated, then said it softly, like she was afraid I'd bolt if she pushed too hard. "That's why your story is so important. Because of your... your dad."

My throat closed. For a moment I couldn't think, couldn't breathe. "Yeah," I managed. "He... his accident—but it was in the news… it was an accident." Did Vanessa think it wasn't? The possibility he'd done it on purpose had crossed my mind many times. I wondered who else had thought the same.

Vanessa tilted her head slightly, sympathy in her expression but another feeling—curiosity, maybe. "Right. I read about that. But—" She hesitated. "Wasn't his body never recovered?"

The question sent a wave of shock sputtering through me. I blinked at her. "What?"

She looked uncomfortable now, like she regretted saying it. "I—sorry, I shouldn't have—"

"No, it's fine," I interrupted quickly, forcing my voice to stay calm even as my mind scrambled. "I... I don't know. I always thought they found him."

"You did?" Her brow furrowed. "I must've mixed it up then." But we both knew it—Vanessa didn't "mix up" the facts. Ever. She did her research and she did it well.

I nodded, too quickly. "Probably. There were a lot of accidents around the same time."

She stared at me for a long time, her mouth open like she was about to say more, but then she decided to drop it. I took a long sip of coffee, trying to hide how badly my hand was shaking. The idea wouldn't leave me. His body never recovered. It didn't make sense. The urn was on the mantle. Surely I'd know if his body hadn't been recovered?

"So," Vanessa said after a long silence, her voice gentler now, "you've been back at the house for a few days?"

I nodded. "Yeah. It's weird being there again. Feels smaller. Like the air's heavier."

She gave a quiet hum of understanding. "I bet. That house… it's been hard anytime I pass it, honestly." She laughed, but it faded quickly. "You know, I always worried about you there."

The words hit differently than they used to. Back in high school, she'd say things in a teasing way—half-joke, half-truth. But now her tone was quieter, more serious.

I looked down at my hands again. "You did?"

"Yeah." She traced a finger along her cup. "You'd come to school looking so tired. And when I asked what was wrong, you'd say you didn't sleep much. Or your dad was in one of his moods."

I stared at her for a long moment. The old walls of the café felt like they were closing in, pressing against me with all the years I'd spent pretending nothing had happened.

"I don't remember saying that," I said quietly.

"You did," she said, her voice steady. "Not a lot, but enough. I figured... I don't know. I was just a kid. I didn't know what to think."

Silence stretched between us again. I felt the pull of it—the way grief and shame mixed, and became too hard to name. I wanted to tell her it was okay, I was fine now, and the past was the past. But the words stuck in my throat.

"I don't think I ever truly understood him," I glanced down at my hands. "When I was little, he was great. He could be so... charming, you know? Everyone thought he was this funny, kind guy. And then he—" I stopped, searching for words that wouldn't sound like I was still that scared teenager. "He changed."

Vanessa nodded, her expression somber. "I remember the look on your face when his truck pulled up outside the school. You'd go quiet."

I closed my eyes for a second, the memory hitting sharper than I expected. "Yeah. He had that effect."

"You ever talk about it? After... everything?"

"No," I said quickly. How could I explain to Vanessa she wasn't the only one I hadn't had contact with? I couldn't tell her my mother had told me not to come home.

We both sat there, not looking at each other. The noise of the café faded until it felt like we were sitting in a little bubble of quiet no one else could see.

"I'm sorry," Vanessa said finally. "I didn't mean to dredge all that up."

"It's okay," I replied. And weirdly, it was. Or at least, it felt like maybe it could be. "I didn't expect it, that's all."

The clock above the counter ticked loudly. Late afternoon sunlight spilled through the café window, catching in Vanessa's hair and turning the edges gold. I watched her for a moment, remembering how she used to braid my hair in study hall, how she once punched a boy for calling me "ugly," how she'd been the only one who ever came over after dark.

"Do you remember," I said suddenly, "the night before graduation? When we sat out by the lake?"

She smiled faintly. "Yeah. You said you wanted to leave and never come back."

"I can't believe I ever said that. I know I didn't mean it," I murmured.

She studied my quietly but didn't respond. The tension seemed to have eased between us.

"If you ever wanted to talk about it—anything... I'm around."

"Thanks," I said. But I half wondered if she meant personally or for her article.

Outside, the air was colder than I expected. The cozy warmth of the café and a hot drink had made me forget. I shivered as I tucked my arms around myself and rushed to my car.

For a moment, I imagined my father's truck sinking beneath that surface—the headlights cutting through the murky water, the bubbles rising and vanishing. I told myself I remembered him being dragged from the lake, the funeral home, the urn.

But Vanessa's words wouldn't leave me. They played in my head over and over.

His body was never recovered. *His body was never recovered.*

A chill ran down my spine. Why had I never known this?

CHAPTER TWENTY-ONE

I LEFT BLEEDING Brews feeling like a cloud was hanging over my head. Vanessa's questions had dragged up a lot of painful memories about my father. I barely remembered driving home and I drifted up to my bedroom, almost driven by an invisible force. In my old bedroom, I started digging around in my closet before I found what I was looking for.

Pulling my old gym bag down from the top shelf, I brushed off a thin layer of dust and carried it over to the bed. It felt heavier than I remembered, as though weighted not with the things in it but with time. When I unzipped it, the scent of old paper and cotton candy body spray drifted out, and suddenly the years seemed to fold back on themselves.

Inside were my high school yearbooks, a few worn notebooks, a scrapbook, and stacks of folded notes passed between friends. I dumped everything out across the bed, then sank down beside the pile, curling up as the memories washed over me.

Most of the high school notes would be to or from

Vanessa. I brushed past the older notes from junior high we had passed around to a circle of friends. Sorting them out quickly, I was surprised to realize how quickly I recognize everyone's handwriting.

Violet Marshall's block letters on one note made me smile. I hadn't thought of her since she'd moved away in the ninth grade. For a moment, I wondered where she was now and if she still wore thick swooping black eyeliner. I smiled to myself. Will Porter's writing on one note made me think about the massive crush I'd had on him for three years before he'd asked me to the tenth grade homecoming dance.

Those memories felt like an entirely different lifetime. The one where I'd started pretending I lived a normal life. Maybe I'd never stopped pretending.

I built a stack of notes between me and Vanessa and began unfolding them. Most of them were silly things about the boys in class, stupid teachers, or the snobby girls.

But then:

Hey, are you okay? You don't look so good today??!!?! XO-Van

Oh my god Van, last night was the worst. My dad was really mad at me for leaving my sneakers in the doorway. I guess he tripped and fell but I didn't do it on purpose! I ran upstairs to try to hide in my room, but he followed me. He almost never comes up there anymore. But when I heard him stomping up the stairs, I wanted to cry. I can't believe I'm even telling you because it's so embarrassing. He was so drunk. My mother stuck up for me, like usual but they got into a fight and he almost shoved her down the stairs. She barely caught herself. I could tell she was scared, but it must have scared him too, because he went back downstairs right after that. I didn't go back down last night at all.

I'm so sorry Grace! I'm here 4 u though, ok? You know you're basically like my sister. Plus you know you can come stay the night at my house anytime you want, right?

That note got me thinking. When I was little, my dad's anger had all been directed at my mother. I learned early how to disappear. I'd tuck myself behind my bedroom door, knees pulled tight to my chest, counting the seconds between shouts. That rhythm became my heartbeat—one, two, three, SMASH. Silence. Then her voice, low and trembling but still protective, always protective.

But when I got older, things shifted. There were nights he turned his anger toward me. I could see it building—the way his jaw would tighten, the way his eyes would cloud over, as if he was looking at something far away that he hated more than me. But before he could step closer, my mother would move. Always. She'd step between us like a shield, her hands raised, her body trembling but firm. She took the words meant for me, the blows meant for me. She'd whisper for me to go to my room, to lock the door, to wait.

The next morning, she'd pretend everything was fine. She'd brush her hair to hide the bruise, hum softly as she made breakfast, and smile when she caught me watching her. "It's okay," she'd say. "You're safe." But I wasn't stupid. Safety was borrowed, not owned—she bought it for me with pieces of herself.

My father's moods were weather systems—unpredictable, violent, and always coming back. My mother's courage, though, was the constant. It was quiet, not the kind that shouts or fights back. It was the kind that endures.

After he left for work or passed out on the couch, she'd come into my room and sit beside me. We didn't talk about what had happened; we didn't need to. She'd run her fingers through my hair and whisper stories—about the sea, about running away to a warmer state, a safer state. I used to believe her. I think she wanted to believe it herself too.

CHAPTER TWENTY-TWO

I'D FALLEN asleep on the pile of notes and memorabilia, so I woke up in the morning with a stiff neck. I made my way downstairs to get a cup of coffee. Pulling on a sweater and sneakers, I stood at the backdoor, gazing out into the backyard.

Gardening was such an interesting hobby for my mother to pick up. I'd never known her to be very outdoorsy. But she *had* mentioned in her journal she would need a hobby after I left. I didn't know she'd always wanted a garden, but for the first time, I took the time to visually examine and appreciate every bush and plant.

Unlocking the backdoor, I set my coffee cup down and stepped outside. The air was thick with the scent of rain and earth, a damp promise of a storm on its way in. For a moment, it was just me, the gray sky, and the garden my mother had tended for the last… who knew how many years.

She'd obviously loved this little patch of land more than people. Rows of wilted goldenrod lined the fence, their yellow heads bowed as though in mourning. The pink and orange coneflowers had gone pale, and then the crab apple tree stood in the middle like a shrine. The small apples hung from the branches, and dozens of them littered the ground underneath.

I shoved my hands in my sweatshirt pocket and stared at that tree. It looked wrong, like it had grown at a bad angle or was distorted beneath the bark. The longer I looked, the more a faint unease coiled in my chest.

Maybe it was the weather. The clouds had turned an ominous gray, letting me know the storm was imminent. A shiver rolled through me. I swore I could hear the faintest hum coming from the direction of the crab apple tree—a low vibration, like the whisper of bees, though there weren't any bees this time of year.

I took a few steps toward it.

The ground squished beneath my shoes. I paused halfway down the garden path, the smell of wet soil turning sharp, metallic. My stomach twisted. I told myself I was being ridiculous. It was a tree. A tree and nothing more.

Then the first drop of rain fell, the sudden coolness of it hitting the back of my neck. It was followed by another, then another, until a light drizzle surrounded me. The sound should have been comforting, but it wasn't. My vision swam for a second, and I reached up to rub at my temple. That's when it hit—a sharp pain, sudden and electric, like a flashbulb had gone off inside my skull. The smell of lilacs was so strong, it was suffocating. The garden blurred.

Everything went black.

And then I was in a different place.

The smell hit first—motor oil, and the sharp, bitter scent of whiskey. Then came the sound: my father's voice, loud and slurred, bouncing off the walls like a ricochet.

"Useless," he spat. "You think you can walk away from me?"

I wasn't seeing him so much as *feeling* him. His anger filled every corner, seeping under my skin, into my bones. I saw flashes: the kitchen, the broken tray, my mother's face pale with fear. My own voice tried to speak, but it was like shouting underwater.

Then, louder than before, his words tore through the dream like a blade. "You'll come back. You *always* come back."

The words echoed, reverberating until they didn't sound like his anymore. They became more and more distorted, like a monster in slow motion.

Then silence, all at once.

And I woke up.

I was lying on the wet grass, the rain coming down in thin silver sheets. My body ached, and my head throbbed where it had hit the ground. For a moment, I couldn't remember how I'd gotten there. The crab apple tree loomed above me, its branches dripping. I was shaking from the cold.

Then I heard it. Faint, but unmistakable.

"Useless."

My heart pounded in my chest as I scrambled to my feet, looking wildly around. There was no one there. But I'd have swore my father had said it.

The garden was dark in the late morning fog. My clothing was soaking through and I was coated in mud. I scrambled back in the backdoor, into the warmth. Pulling off my sweatshirt, shivering in my thin T-shirt, I kicked off my shoes.

A loud knock at the door, and I froze. The sound came again, deliberate—almost urgent. I sighed to myself. Changing my pants would have to wait. I went to the front door and opened it.

An older woman stood there, holding a huge umbrella that was dripping all around her. Her lips were in a tight, polite smile but it didn't reach her eyes.

"Hello. I'm Mrs. Dowell. You must be… Heidi's daughter. I live a couple houses down the road." She gestured into the rain. Her voice sounded strained.

I blinked, still disoriented, trying to piece together why she might be here. I cocked my head to the side for a second, eyes narrowed. "Mrs. Dowell…" I repeated, trying to place it. She nodded and I snapped my fingers, making her jump.

"Oh, sorry," I laughed. "I remember you!" But I stopped short there, because what I remembered was how she was a rude, busybody and my mother hated her. She'd moved onto our street my senior year of high school, and my mother had gone out of her way to avoid her.

She nodded, lowering her umbrella. The rain had slowed down and she was under the porch awning. "I was friends with your mother. She was lovely. I'm so sorry to hear about what happened. Such a shame." She made a sound between her teeth and I had to work to avoid visibly cringing.

Her eyes wandered over my shoulder. "I hope this isn't

a bad time." She looked back down at my pants, which were covered in mud and soaking wet.

"I was out in the garden and got caught in the downpour. I was already wet, so I didn't rush in, but… it's pretty chilly out there." I found myself saying. I certainly wasn't about to announce I'd blacked out and dreamt of my father yelling at me.

"Such a shame though, your mother," she repeated, looking at me expectantly. I wasn't sure what she was getting at.

"Your mother, she always deserved better." Her tone made the hairs on my neck stand up. She shifted her umbrella to the other hand and leaned in like she was about to tell me a secret.

"I know it must be difficult—losing both of your parents. And coming back here after all this time. I don't think I ever saw you around after your father passed. Must've been what… Ten, twelve years ago?"

I blinked, my mouth too dry to respond.

"Well, anyway, time sure does fly. And your father—Patrick, wasn't it? He was such a character, eh?" The way she said his name—like it was a filthy cuss word—made my stomach knot up.

"I didn't ever get to know him too well, but you hear things… through the grapevine. Your mother sure put up with a lot." She paused, her eyes darting toward mine. "Did you know I saw him once? He was out in the yard yelling about… well, I don't know what exactly. No one was here, but he was shouting away. Quite a temper, your father had."

The blood drained from my face. I forced a laugh that came out sounding like a cough.

"People do like their gossip, don't they?"

"Oh, yes, they sure do," she agreed. "I didn't mean to bring up bad memories. I think your mother was a saint, putting up with all that. And you—well, you look like you've turned out…" She struggled to find the right word, looking at me, soaked and muddy. "Okay."

"I'm fine." I nodded, and she smiled then, a genuine one.

"That's good to hear." She patted my arm. "Well, I guess I better get back home, looks like the rain let up—for now at least."

"Thanks for stopping by," I said politely, although I wished she hadn't. She turned and her umbrella popped back out.

"Watch those steps," I told her as she avoided the broken steps with a "tut" sound.

As she reached the end of the driveway, a truck pulled in and I was glad to see the handyman's logo on the side of it. I didn't think I could handle any more social visits.

BLEEDING HEARTS VALLEY
BEHAVIORAL HEALTH SERVICES SOUTH

Client Name: Grace Jenkins
10/14/2008
Session Note:
Attempts to discuss blackout episodes were met with push back. Client did not want to engage in this topic. However, client self-reports ongoing episodes of sleepwalking and engaging in various activities while asleep. She describes waking up in different locations of her home and occasionally discovering that she has performed tasks (e.g., eating, rearranging items) with no memory of doing so. She reports these behaviors have been occurring intermittently for several months, though frequency appears to be increasing. Client did confirm that these episodes often occur after a blackout.
Subjective:
Client reports feelings of confusion and concern upon waking, describing the experiences as "scary" and "feeling out of control." She denies any recent significant life stressors. The client denies use of alcohol or recreational drugs and reports no current medications that may impact sleep.
Objective:
Client was alert, oriented, and engaged throughout session. Mood appeared anxious but cooperative. Speech and thought processes were clear and coherent.
Assessment:
Symptoms consistent with parasomnia (sleepwalking disorder), possibly exacerbated by underlying anxiety. Most likely related to blackouts. Further exploration needed.

Practitioner: Peter Aderman,LMSW

CHAPTER TWENTY-THREE

THE HANDYMAN WORKED through the list of projects I had for him fairly quickly. I was grateful when he didn't try to make small talk or be overly friendly. He asked a few questions and got straight to work. By late afternoon, he was packing up his supplies and cleaning up any messes he had made.

I paid him and watched as he headed back to his truck, offering a last casual wave before climbing inside. The knot of tension in my shoulders loosened—at least now I had someone reliable to call if something else was wrong. I returned the wave, went back inside, and slid the lock into place behind me.

I'd changed clothes while he worked outside, but a shower hadn't felt like a good idea with someone coming in and out of the house. As soon as his truck pulled away, I'd taken the stairs two at a time, the bathroom door shutting behind me with a sense of relief.

Standing in the hot water, I finally had a chance to reflect back on what had happened in the garden that morning. I'd pushed it to the back of my mind, but as I showered and toweled off, I let my mind replay the dream and waking up. The voice I thought I'd heard when I woke up had probably been an echo from my dream. My brain was still foggy at that point.

As I slipped into a pair of sweatpants and an oversized sweatshirt, a knock rattled the front door. *Who could possibly be here now?*

The second knock was harder, louder. Almost aggressive. I bounded down the steps, still toweling my hair off.

With a quick peek out the side window, I recognized Thomas's truck. Heat flared in my chest, sharp and sudden, my jaw tightening as my hands involuntarily curled into fists. Why was he back? Couldn't he take a hint? Or a direct order?

"What do you want?" I snapped as I swung the door open. Thomas nearly snarled back at me but quickly rearranged his face into what I was sure he thought was friendly.

"Sorry to bother you—looks like I caught you at a bad time, but I had to tell you…" I held up a hand to stop him.

"You didn't *have to* tell me a single thing. There's nothing you could tell me that I *need* to know."

"Well, I…" He paused, taking a deep breath. "Okay, that's probably true, but you very well might *want* to know this."

I dropped the towel I'd been using on my hair on the side table and crossed my arms, giving him a look.

"Can I come in?" The man did not take a hint. Either he couldn't read body language at all, or he didn't care.

"No, you may not. Whatever you think I want to hear, you can tell me right here. Otherwise, you can leave." Adrenaline surged through me—the power of being so direct making me feel more like myself. At least the 'myself' I was familiar with now. City Grace. I couldn't let being back home turn me into a pushover.

Thomas shifted his weight back and forth. He looked like he was weighing his options, as limited as they were.

"Alright." He finally nodded. "Now I know you said you weren't interested in selling. But I felt like you'd want to know this. The city has agreed to allow a certain portion of this neighborhood to be rezoned as commercial property. Due to the size of this property specifically, it's in high demand among several investors." He paused to see my reaction but I was already rolling my eyes.

"Okay, well I can see you're not impressed but the investors are offering a lot more than I originally thought. It's almost double—for your property specifically. Otherwise they'd have to buy two other properties on this street to build the apartment building they're planning," he prattled on.

"I'm still not interested, Thomas." I moved to close the door.

"Wait—you could even have first dibs on one of the apartments, if you're not wanting to leave the neighborhood, although with the amount of the purchase, I don't know why you'd stay over here when you could move to one of the nicer developments. Maybe Fringed?"

"I like this neighborhood. Why would I want to move over there?"

"Right, so one of the apartments then..." He was continuing to try to inject positivity into his voice, but I could tell he was getting irritated. *Good, that makes two of us.*

"Okay, I'm only telling you this one last time. I am *not* interested. I am not selling. I will not be selling. And I don't want you on my property again. Not when I'm home or when I'm not. This is becoming harassment, and the next time you step foot on my property, I *will* file a restraining order. Now please, leave." Thomas blinked, his mouth flubbering open, trying to think of one more thing to say.

"You'll regret it," he hissed as I closed the door in his face, which was contorted with barely restrained anger.

After overhearing his conversation with those two men, I knew he thought this was his ticket out, but selling the house wasn't an option.

Out the back window, a crab apple fell from the tree.

No, selling this place was definitely *not* an option.

CHAPTER TWENTY-FOUR

AFTER A QUICK CALL to the nursing home confirmed Aunt Clara was cleared to accept visitors, I scrambled to get ready to go. I wanted to bring a gift, but I couldn't decide what was safe—and wouldn't trigger her. After a quick inventory of ingredients, I decided on chocolate chip cookies—because my aunt and I always made them when I was at her house as a kid.

I threw together a batch quickly. While I waited for them to cool, I finished getting dressed. Tucking the still warm cookies into a large container, I headed out to the car. I made a quick stop through a drive through to grab lunch before heading in the right direction.

Once I pulled back into the parking lot of White Oak Manor for the second time, I tucked the container of cookies under my arm and made my way to the door. My stomach gurgled and I wished I hadn't scarfed down a cheeseburger from a fast food joint on the way. It was nerves, and I hoped seeing Aunt Clara would calm those nerves. I had no reason to be nervous—did I?

The receptionist recognized me right away and said

she would get Nurse Eva to walk me back. I remained standing in the lobby, waiting.

A text message popped up as I was waiting. Vanessa. We had exchanged numbers but I was still surprised to see her name on my screen. I hadn't expected her to contact me so soon. Clicking on the notification, I opened her message to see that she wanted to meet up again. She suggested we go to the local donut shop, Hole's—one of our old haunts. I agreed to meeting her there, and tucked my phone back into my pocket as the nurse came into the lobby.

"Hello! Ms. Jenkins, it's nice to see you. Clara is doing so much better, but we are going to be on alert today. I know you will be giving her very upsetting news, so I'll be on stand-by, but I don't want to hover." She was leading me down a hallway with a beautiful mural painted on it. I ran my hand over it and she turned back and smiled. "Our residents helped paint that." I was impressed.

"So this is the nurses' station—" She held her hand out to the left where a small desk area was set up. "And your aunt's room is right here…" She turned back to me. Two doors down, the door was slightly ajar.

I wanted to ask her to slow down, to give me a minute to prepare myself, but she walked right to the door and pushed it open gently.

"Clara, you have a visitor." Nurse Eva was already in the room and I was forced to follow. Aunt Clara was sitting in an arm chair by the window, a tiny, withered version of her old self. Her hair, salt and pepper the last time I'd seen her, was now fluffy white. Her skin was wrinkled and she looked like she had shrunk sizes—not just weight lost but everything about her seemed small and fragile.

Aunt Clara stared at me for a moment, and then her mouth twisted before she said, "Heidi?" And then she paused and cocked her head before I could correct her. "No, not Heidi… but you look like her. Yes, just like her. So much like her," she rambled, and then stared out the window.

I swallowed the lump in my throat. I'd avoided thinking about how much I'd noticed my features resembling my mother's as I grew older. It had been just a matter of time before someone bluntly pointed it out.

"I'll leave you two to it. Call out if you need anything, I'll be right out at my desk," Nurse Eva said and stepped out of the room.

"Aunt Clara…" My voice cracked and she turned abruptly to look at me. "It's me… Grace."

"Grace?" she repeated, as though she'd never heard the name. My heart dropped.

"Heidi's daughter," I whispered.

"Oh, Grace. Heidi's daughter," she repeated flatly.

"Can I sit here?" I asked, pointing to a small side chair. She stared at me blankly so I took it as a yes and sat down.

"I made you cookies." I presented the tupperware to her and lifted the lid. She leaned forward with childlike interest.

"Chocolate chip?" she asked, and when I nodded, she snatched one and sank back in her chair and took a bite. She closed her mind for a minute, chewing with a slight smile at the corners of her mouth.

"Me and my niece used to make chocolate chip cookies. That was so long ago," she said, and I blinked rapidly, willing away the tears that threatened to fall.

"I'm your niece, Aunt Clara. It's me, Grace."

Aunt Clara looked at me then, like she was actually

seeing me, and not looking through me. She reached out her hand and touched my cheek.

"It is you, isn't it? Why are you here?" I couldn't tell if she was having a moment of clarity or not, because her voice was still very dreamlike.

"I wanted to see you. I've missed you." My voice broke and I reached out for her hand. She let me cover her tiny, frail hand with mine. For a moment, she smiled.

"Oh Gracie, you've grown up. But why are you here? After that night. You can't be here. Oh no, where's Heidi?" She stood up, shuffling her feet and began pacing next to the window.

I swallowed hard. "That's what I'm here to tell you about." I searched for the right words. Aunt Clara froze and looked at me. She blinked and then began pacing again.

"No, I knew this day would come. I told her. I told her. And now you're back. No one can know. And not the garden. What will you do?" She stopped abruptly again and looked at me for a moment before resuming her pacing.

"Aunt Clara, can you... would you mind sitting down for a minute?" I asked gently. I was surprised when she did.

"I have to tell you about Mom. I have bad news." I sighed.

"What happened to your mom? Where's Heidi?" She looked over my shoulder and then back at me.

"Mom had... an incident. She... Mom had a heart attack. She didn't make it." I reached up to swipe at the tears that were falling now.

"Didn't make it?" Her voice was shrill. She stood up again. "What about the house? The garden? No one can know." Aunt Clara paced back, wringing her hands through her hair. It stuck out in tufts around her face.

Her voice was getting higher pitched and I stood up, bumping against the chair. I almost fell over. Catching myself, I stepped backwards. Next to me was her dresser with the old jewelry box that used to sit on the dresser at her own place. Without thinking I lifted the lid, and the familiar tune whirled on. Glancing over, I hoped the sound would be calming to Aunt Clara, but she didn't even seem to notice.

I reached into the jewelry box, shifting her necklaces and bracelets around. I remembered the jewelry had a false bottom and I wondered if she'd stored anything valuable in it. Checking the door to her room quickly, I pushed on one side to slide out the bottom and was surprised to see a thin notebook wedged in there.

Aunt Clara stopped babbling behind me and I turned. She was staring at me, her mouth opening and shutting like a fish out of water. Lifting the notebook, I looked back at her and thumbed it open. It was a journal, although from the quick flip through, a lot of it was illegible.

Aunt Clara suddenly started squawking loudly, coming over and shutting the jewelry box quickly. She didn't try to take the journal from me, so I stood there holding it.

"No one can find out. No one. No one. The house. Leave it alone. No one." Aunt Clara's voice was getting loud and loud until she was shrieking. I turned to get a nurse, but Nurse Eva was already rushing in the door, a syringe in one hand. I slipped the journal into my pocket and stepped back out of the way.

"I'm so sorry," I mumbled, but the nurse ushered me out, murmuring comforting words.

I stood out in the hall until Nurse Eva and an orderly got Aunt Clara back in her bed.

"I'm so sorry," I apologized again when Nurse Eva stepped out in the hallway. "I told her about my mother."

"It's okay, I expected her to get upset. Hopefully she calms down quicker than the last episode. Getting upset might be a good sign—it means she understood what you told her." I nodded but I was sick to my stomach.

It seemed like Aunt Clara was trying to tell me something but I was shaking, unable to think clearly. I slipped out of the building, suddenly eager to be alone.

Back in the car, I sat behind the wheel, trying to collect myself. My hands were still trembling, so I pressed them flat against my thighs and focused on breathing, slow and deliberate, the way I'd once been told to do. The echoes of my aunt's voice—sharp, fractured, not quite tethered to reality—kept replaying in my head, each burst of sound tightening my chest all over again. I stared through the windshield without really seeing anything, letting the silence settle. It was really just me. Aunt Clara may still be here physically, but she was gone in every other sense. The thought landed heavily, and I swallowed hard, blinking back tears until the world steadied.

After a moment, I wiped my face, straightened my shoulders, and reached for the seatbelt, not because I was ready to leave, but because I needed something normal, something solid, to hold onto.

Pulling the journal out of my pocket and clicking the belt in place, I opened it to the first entry. The first few lines were written fairly neatly, but then the pen dug into the paper, poking small holes and the writing got more frantic, sliding down the page, getting bigger and repeating itself.

Anyone seeing it would think it made no sense whatsoever and was the ramblings of a mentally disturbed individual. I flipped through the journal and the rest of it was similar. There didn't seem to be a single useful entry to help me understand what was going on. Sighing, I tossed it on the passenger seat and started the engine.

4/10/2015

So many secrets. So many. All the secrets. I will keep the secret though. For Heidi. I'd do anything for my baby sister. I know how much this means to her. And yes. It's a secret. I have to keep it.

secret

secret

Shhhhh

Don't tell, Don't tell Clara!!!!! Don't. Shhh. It's a secret. It's a secret. It's a secret. It's a secret. It's a secret. It's a secret. It's a secret. It's a secret.

SECRET

SECRET

SECRET

IT'S A SECRET. Don't tell. Don't tell the secret.

CHAPTER TWENTY-FIVE

I DIDN'T HAVE time to go home before meeting Vanessa at Hole's, so I drove around and checked out the things that had changed since I was last in town. It felt like a lot, and yet overall, nothing had changed.

Parking in front of Hole's and opening the car door, I could smell that heavy scent of sugar and cocoa. My mouth watered, ready to devour one of their giant donuts. I hoped they hadn't changed a single thing. Their donuts came as a pair—the big donut one flavor, and the hole being a coordinating flavor.

I swung open the door, relieved to see I'd beat Vanessa there this time. I could look over the menu without feeling rushed. The shop was pretty empty, which was fortunate since they only had a few small tables. The girl at the register couldn't have been more than seventeen and I smiled at her as I stepped up to the counter.

"I would love to try this new flavor—the coconut cake donut with the strawberry stuffed donut hole."

"Oh that one is so good! Do you want a drink?"

"Sure, I'll have a regular hot cocoa, for here." I gestured

toward the tables. After ringing me up, she let me know I could have a seat and she would bring it to my table.

The little bell on the door rang and I turned as Vanessa breezed in as I was about to sit down.

"Hey!" She greeted me with a small wave. "I'm gonna order real quick." I nodded and waited for her to join me.

"I love how this place hasn't changed," I said to her as she sat down. She looked around like she was seeing it for the first time.

"I hate to admit it, but I haven't even been here in months. And to come in and sit down—no… haven't done that since high school." She paused, and I lifted an eyebrow. She shrugged. "I definitely pick them up and go home and binge on them at night now after a rough work-day." I laughed with her and we waited while the cashier brought us our donuts and cocoas.

I sank my teeth into my donut, wondering how this could taste like a donut and coconut cake at exactly the same time. I didn't even glance at what Vanessa ordered—I'd probably want that next. We made idle chitchat and then Vanessa set down her cup and looked at me like she had big news. I set my cup down too and waited.

"I hate to keep bringing this up." She looked at me, like she was trying to figure out how to say what she wanted to say. She sighed and leaned forward. "Look, I couldn't help but notice when I mentioned your dad last time, it seemed like you didn't know his body was never recovered. And I didn't want to upset you, but I've done a ton of research about this, but when they pulled his truck from Moon Lake, he wasn't in it. They assumed he got out of the cab—the window was down—but they weren't able to find his body."

She stopped there and looked at me. My hands trembled as I reached for my cocoa and I took a slow sip, avoiding her eyes. Setting the cup back down, I tucked my hands under the table on my lap so she couldn't see how much they were shaking.

"I… yeah, you're right. I didn't know." There was no point in lying to Vanessa. I never had been able to, and there was no reason to start now anyway. "I guess I was surprised, but I didn't know—because I went back to school, I mean everything was a blur when it happened, and then I never asked about it. I assumed. I think I was in shock… it didn't occur to me."

"Hey, it's okay, you were only nineteen," Vanessa said, looking at me pointedly. She still knew me better than anyone.

"Yeah. Ever since you said that, I have been avoiding thinking about it because I feel bad I didn't know. I mean, I don't have any reason to feel guilty about not asking more —I was in shock and would never have thought to ask that. But still…"

"I get it." She nodded. "I've been talking to a lot of families whose loved ones were never found. I'm almost sorry I was the one to tell you because I think it's easier for people to grieve and accept it when the body is recovered."

I didn't say anything. I couldn't admit the truth. When my mom woke me up the morning after my father's accident to tell me, my first feeling was relief. Questions about his body or the accident had never occurred to me to ask, because I hadn't cared. All I knew was my mom was going to be safe and I didn't have to worry about her while I was away at school.

But suddenly, I *did* want to know. This felt like another secret my mother had kept, although it wasn't intentional. I was annoyed I didn't have the internet at home.

I rushed through the rest of our visit, changing the subject and trying to keep it lighthearted. I didn't even feel guilty when I made an excuse about being tired and needing to get home.

Outside, in my car, I tried to do a search on my phone, but every time a headline popped up that I wanted to open, I hit a paywall. Glancing at the time, I had another couple of hours before the library closed.

I made sure Vanessa had driven away before making a U-turn to head toward the library.

CHAPTER TWENTY-SIX

THE PARKING LOT of the BHV Library was half-empty when I pulled in, the evening sky darkening. The building looked older than I remembered—bricks darkened by years of rain, the carved letters above the entrance softened and moss-lined.

Shoving my keys into my pocket as I stepped out of the car, the smell of asphalt overwhelmed me in the misty air.

Inside, the lobby was warm, dry, and smelled faintly of old paper and lemon polish. A banner for the *Local History Archives* hung near the stairwell, its corners curling. I followed the signs down a narrow corridor to the basement level, where the lights were dimmer and the air cooler. It was the kind of place where sound didn't travel properly—footsteps were muffled, and there were no echoes.

A woman sat behind the reference desk, peering at a monitor through glasses. Her hair was silver and clipped short, shiny under the glow of her desk lamp. When she looked up, her expression softened into a mix between curiosity and kindness.

"Can I help you find anything?" she asked, her voice gentle but steady.

"I hope so," I said. "I'm looking for newspaper archives. Around November, thirteen years ago. There was an accident—well, a disappearance. Out near Moon Lake."

Her eyes flicked up at me again, a flicker of interest—only heavier. "You must mean the Jenkins' case," she said quietly.

The sound of my last name hung in the air. "Yes," I said. "That was my father. Patrick Jenkins."

Her lips parted slightly. She drew in a breath. "Oh, my goodness." For a moment, she looked at me, eyes tracing my face, recognizing a familiarity. "You're—well, you must be Grace."

I nodded, surprised. "Did you know my mother?"

She smiled, but it was the kind of smile that comes after a painful memory. "We went to high school together. Heidi—your mom—and I weren't close, exactly, but I knew her."

That past tense tugged at me, quiet and unavoidable. I shifted my weight, then said softly, "She passed away a couple weeks ago."

The woman blinked, and her expression collapsed for a moment. "Oh, honey, I'm so sorry." Her hand went to her necklace. "I hadn't heard. She used to come in, to look through the historical fiction section."

"She did love to read when she had the time…"

The woman nodded slowly. "I'm Anne. I work with the historical collection downstairs. You're welcome to look through the newspaper archives. We have digital copies, which are very easy to search."

She stood. "Come on," she said. "I'll show you."

Anne guided me to a computer with a huge outdated

monitor. Quickly, she showed me how to search the *Bleeding Hearts Chronicle* archives. "Here, these are all the articles for that entire month of November—and then you'll want to click here to see December." She showed me where to click.

I thanked her and she paused. "I don't know what you're looking for, but I hope you find it." I smiled and she patted me on the shoulder before turning and leaving me alone.

The computer whirred loudly, and I wondered how old it was exactly. The monitor was not a modern clear screen—the text was all grainy, but still legible. I scrolled as the screen flickered.

"Truck Found Submerged in Moon Lake—Driver Missing After Storm."

The article was short. I soaked it up, searching for any little clue. Local authorities had been called to the lake after a witness spotted the tailgate of a silver pickup near the shoreline at dawn. The license plate matched my father's. Divers searched for two days but found nothing—no body, no sign of a struggle. Police said the rain had made the roads slick and visibility poor; they believed he must have misjudged the curve and gone off the embankment.

There was a grainy photograph of the truck being pulled from the water, headlights like blind eyes. My heart seemed to catch, almost pausing. I'd never seen this article. Never seen this photo. I wiped my palms off on my pants. They were slick with sweat, making it difficult to control the mouse.

I scrolled further down until I found another article about it.

"Police Looking For Witnesses After Jenkins Disappearance."

According to that article, two motorists had called in around the time the storm peaked. One said they'd seen headlights near the waterline—too close. The other claimed they'd heard shouting, though the wind and rain made it hard to tell. The police requested anyone with information to come forward.

I frowned. Witnesses… So did they think my father could still be alive? *Could he still be alive now?* I'd always assumed no one knew anything else.

Or… could someone have killed my father. Pushed him in the lake and his truck after? Who could he have been arguing with? My thoughts flashed to the love letter from Phillip, sitting in my mom's box of cherished cards and letters. Then I remembered the last thing my father had ever said to me. *You think you know everything. Your mother ain't no saint.*

What if my father knew about the affair and confronted Phillip? What if Phillip killed my father and then made it all look like an accident. I sat up a little straighter.

I kept scrolling until I found another mention.

"Anonymous Tip Leads Search to Northern Shore in Jenkins Case—No Evidence Found".

The article was only a couple of paragraphs long. Clearly the investigation was already petering by then. A tip had been called in from an untraceable number. The caller claimed they'd seen a figure walking along the north shore after midnight, soaking and limping. Police investigated but found no footprints, no trace of anyone. The article ended with a phrase that made my heart lurch. *Authorities have not ruled out the possibility that Jenkins survived the accident.*

My throat constricted and I struggled to swallow, to breathe. I forced air in, making myself cough. Survived? My mind raced. I couldn't make sense of it but this had to be related to my mother telling me not to come back home. I just knew it.

My hand shaking, I continued to scroll down until I found another mention.

"Jenkins Family Thanks Officials—Investigation Continues"

There was a quote from my mother. *"We want closure. We trust the police investigation, headed up by Detective Andrews, are doing everything they can."* Closure. Something I'd never had. Now I might never get it.

When I finally stopped scrolling, my eyes burned from straining to read the old screen. The clock on the wall said 8:42. They closed at 9PM, but I hadn't noticed the time passing by.

Anne appeared in the doorway, holding up two mugs.

"I thought you might be able to use a cup of tea?" She offered one of them to me. "It's chamomile."

I accepted the mug, wrapping my fingers around it and bringing it to my face, letting the steam warm me. "Thank you, that's really sweet." I took a sip even though tea wasn't my thing and my stomach was churning. She'd taken the time to bring me a cup, I couldn't ignore it.

She sat in the chair beside me. "Did you find what you were looking for?"

"I found… the articles. Maybe more questions than answers." I smiled and shrugged. I could tell she hoped I'd want to chat more about it but I was suddenly sluggish with the weight of everything.

"Thank you so much for your help. I'm going to get out of your hair. Have a great night. Oh and thanks for the tea!" I set the mug down on the desk and gathered myself before rushing back out into the cold air to make the drive home while I was still alert enough.

CHAPTER TWENTY-SEVEN

THE NEXT MORNING, the very first phone call I received was the one I had been dreading. I stared at my phone for a moment before answering, already knowing what it would be about.

A calm, professional voice on the other end said, "We're calling to let you know that your mother's remains are ready for pickup." The word *ready* landed strangely, like it belonged to an ordinary errand rather than this moment.

I remember saying something automatic—"Okay," or "Thank you"—while my brain lagged behind the conversation. They explained the hours, the location, and asked if I had any questions. I didn't. I couldn't think of a single thing to ask.

When the call ended, I sat there holding my phone, feeling like I'd just woken up inside someone else's life. Suddenly, it all felt more real than it had the day before. I wanted to go pick them up immediately, just to get it over with, to stop the waiting. At the same time, I wanted to avoid it forever, because going there would mean accepting that this was final—that there was no more pretending this wasn't happening.

I couldn't leave first thing anyway because I had to wait for the internet provider to come hook up services. I wondered what I was doing exactly. Was I planning on staying? And for how long? I'd never intended to stay more than a couple of weeks, but now something was pulling me home—telling me not to leave.

As I sat frozen, another thought crept in: all the questions I had about my father, about what really happened back then. So much I'd never asked, so much I'd never known, and now, in a way, she was "coming home"—or at least coming back to the space I associated with her. But in an urn.

The morning passed quickly and I was relieved to finally have internet service. I logged into my laptop and connected my phone to the WiFi. *Ahhh internet. Service.* I could have kissed the ground the technician walked on. I sorted through my work emails and felt like I was making a good pathway. I sent an email to my boss, letting her know I was going to start back working remotely the following day and would spend today catching up on all the old emails to sort out what needed to be done.

I hadn't even realized how much time had passed until I glanced at my phone and realized it was after 2PM. Getting myself together, I slowly made my way out to the car.

The drive to Brown's Funeral Home was so much shorter than I needed. I circled around the block a few times before pulling into a parking spot. I wasn't ready—my body buzzed with an energy I couldn't identify, and my hands were numb. I stepped out of the car and stood there, staring at the building.

Everything in my body wanted to duck back. I wanted to race back home and crawl under my covers and hide in my bed. I wanted this all to be a dream I would suddenly wake up from.

But it wasn't, and they were expecting me so I forced myself to go in. The lobby was too quiet—I could hear my own heartbeat. The dim lighting cast shadows on the outdated carpet. The furniture was all ornately carved benches and chairs with burgundy covers.

Music fluted out from a hidden speaker, soft instrumental tunes. A guestbook lay open on the entryway table, a pen next to it, waiting for the next person to sign in. I paused. Was I supposed to? Shrugging, I decided to skip it.

"Can I help you?" A deep voice made me swivel around as a short older gentleman came up behind the little desk at the front.

"Yes, I'm here to pick up my mother's… cremains… I mean, I'm… um—I'm Grace Jenkins." I struggled to find the right words.

"Oh Ms. Jenkins, yes. I'm so sorry for your loss. I'm Gavin Brown. I have a few things for you to sign. We can go into my office here," he said and led me through a door.

I sank into one of the chairs as he slipped behind the desk. It was weird to see brochures and binders with photos of caskets and urns sitting around in an office. Absent-mindedly, I thumbed through one of the brochures and was surprised you could get urns in all kinds of shapes and sizes. Gavin cleared his throat and I glanced up.

"Oh sorry." I crossed my hands in my lap, feeling like I

was supposed to be doing something, but I didn't know what.

"It's okay, don't apologize. As I mentioned on the phone, your mother's attorney handled all the details—well apparently your mother had already made all these plans so you wouldn't have to worry about it, I suppose. So she selected the urn herself. But of course you're free to choose any of these others instead." He pointed to the brochure.

I shook my head vigorously. "Oh no, I want to go with whatever she wanted. That's fine." He nodded, satisfied, and pulled out the paperwork to go over.

After signing everything, he excused himself for a minute to gather everything and returned with a large beige box. It looked like a gift box, sans the ribbon of course.

Lifting the lid, he showed me the urn nestled in a foam insert.

"Okay," I said. But he looked at me like he was expecting more. "That looks great," I added and then I did actually look at the urn and what my mother had chosen. It was the outline of a woman holding a little girl's hand. Engraved underneath was my mother's name and "until we meet again."

I ran my finger over the line and then nodded, putting the lid back on the box.

"Thank you." I lifted the box. "I appreciate everything…"

"Oh, of course. Let me see you out." Gavin led me back to the lobby and opened the door for me. I nodded as I slipped back out into the cold and hurried to my car.

Back in the driver's seat, I set the box on the passenger side and for a moment, I sat there staring at it. This felt so unfuckingreal. I had to keep reminding myself it was all really happening. Turning the car on, I grabbed the seatbelt and pulled it across myself. I wanted so badly to be back home.

The front door clicked shut behind me, and the sound seemed to echo through the empty house. It felt oddly quiet. The box in my hands felt impossibly light for what it held. For who it held.

I carried my mother's remains in and sat down on the couch, lifting the lid again. This time, I took the urn out and held it in my hands, my thumbs rubbing over the etching.

The fireplace mantel waited, its surface already crowded with memories—a clock that hadn't worked in years, a couple picture frames with photos of me as a kid, and, of course, the other urn. My father's.

I set my mother's urn down beside it. The two of them, together again. That would feel comforting to most people. I moved my mother's urn to the other side. My stomach twisted, looking at my father's urn on the other end. I thought about those newspaper articles. *Never recovered a body.*

So what exactly was in his urn? Why do we even have one?

The longer I looked at it, the heavier the room became. The brass caught the afternoon light in dull, uneven reflections. I could see myself in it—a warped, nervous version of me, standing too still.

Now I couldn't stop staring at the seam where the lid met the body. It wasn't sealed like I'd always assumed. A simple twist top. My pulse quickened. I told myself I was being morbid, disrespectful even. I told myself to stop.

But my hand was already reaching out.

The metal was cool under my fingers. For a moment, I hesitated—half expecting a sound, a sign I shouldn't touch the urn. Definitely shouldn't open the urn. I half expected to hear my father yelling at me. But the house remained silent, watching.

I twisted, and the lid made a soft scraping sound.

Holding it in the crook of my arm, I looked down in—darkness. No remains. But a small scrap in the bottom.

A folded up slip of paper sitting there in the bottom like it had been waiting for me. My chest tightened as I reached down and pulled it out.

My hands trembled as I held it, every nerve on edge, every breath shallow and tight. The urn felt impossibly heavy for its size, like it carried decades of unspoken words and unfinished memories. I shoved it back onto the mantle, trying to convince myself it belonged there, that I could stand back and breathe, but my fingers lingered on the cold, smooth surface, reluctant to let go.

I set the lid beside it, feeling the weight of the small, circular thing as if it had a presence of its own, pressing into the silence of the room. My gaze fell on the paper tucked in my hand, a paper that should have been insignificant—but something in my chest told me I couldn't ignore it. I went over to the couch, each step feeling slower, heavier, like wading through thick water, and sank into it. My pulse was loud in my ears, my stomach twisting. I couldn't even imagine what that tiny paper contained, but an instinctual pull said I needed to sit down, to brace myself, to somehow prepare for whatever weight it carried.

As I began to unfold, I noticed my name written on the outside. *Grace,* in my mother's bold writing. My heart lurched, everything feeling fuzzy for a minute. It took me a minute before I could breathe again.

I started unfolding the paper the rest of the way, smoothing it out on my lap, avoiding looking at it.

It wasn't much of a note. A poem. It didn't make sense. At least not to me. The room swayed. I felt like I was suffocating in a field of lilacs. My throat tightened and everything faded to black as the note slipped out of my fingers.

If you have this note, you don't have
me.
Remember, you're the last of the family
tree.
If you need me, I can't be there.
None of this was ever fair.
If you need to know what you can't see,
Just remember the family tree.

CHAPTER TWENTY-EIGHT

NOTHING BUT DARK.

But then, slowly, I hear laughter. The kind that echoes against lockers and tiles. High school. I'm back in high school.

The smell gives it away—the waxy tile floors, the scent of whiteboard markers, that sharp bite of cheap disinfectant. I'm sitting on the low brick wall outside the high school cafeteria, legs swinging, the metal edge biting into the backs of my thighs. Vanessa is next to me, chewing her gum too loudly, a glossy strand of hair tucked behind one ear. She's wearing her infamous denim jacket covered in patches—the one she claimed made her look "mysteriously punk."

We're fifteen. Maybe sixteen. I can feel the sun pressing on my shoulders, hear the basketballs thudding from the gym. Everything looks too bright, like the world was oversaturated.

"Are you okay?" Vanessa asks, tilting her head, squinting at me through the sunlight. "You were quiet in class again."

I want to tell her I'm fine. I want to shrug, make a joke. But I hear myself say instead, "My dad broke a lamp last night."

Her gum chomping stops mid-chew. "What?"

I look down at my hands, picking at the skin around my

thumb. "He got drunk last night. The lamp on the nightstand, the one with the little porcelain flowers? He threw it. It hit the wall. Mom tried to clean it up before I woke up, but there were pieces everywhere."

Vanessa's voice softens. "Does he… do that a lot?"

"Sometimes." I try to sound bored, like I'm talking about the weather. "He gets mad. Yells. Throws things." I swallow hard. Feeling the lie. Down-playing it all significantly.

"What… what does your mom say?"

"Well. Mostly she pretends it's not happening. Tries to protect me. I think she's scared."

Vanessa shifts back and forth nervously. "You should tell someone."

"NO!" A couple of other students turn to us, suddenly interested. I lower my voice. "No, who would I tell? It'll get back to him and he'll know it was me. It would make things worse. For me and for my mom."

The bell rings in the distance but neither of us move.

Then the scene tilts, like the film reel skipping. The light changes—yellow to dim gray—and I'm not outside anymore. I'm in the living room.

He's there. My father.

He's pacing, shouting, although I can't make out the words. His face is red, his words blurred like static. My mother stands near the kitchen doorway, holding a dish towel, eyes wide and wet. I can feel my heart pounding even though I'm only watching, not really there. The air smells like beer and sweat. Glass breaks—and I flinch even though I'm only remembering.

Then I hear my voice again, younger, trembling. "Stop it! Just stop!"

His head snaps toward me. That look—sharp, feral, like I'd dared interrupt the storm. For a second, I think he might come at me. But he doesn't. He turns, slams the door, and leaves. The silence afterward feels louder than his shouting ever did.

I can hear my mother crying softly. I want to go to her, but I can't move. The memory freezes, edges flickering.

Then—it all flickers again.

But we've fast-forwarded about four years. My hands look older. My dorm room is small and cluttered, with clothes on the chair and books stacked like little towers. Thanksgiving break had ended—I can see the empty suitcase on the floor. The phone keeps ringing, vibrating against the desk.

I don't want to answer it. But I do.

"Hey," Vanessa says, her voice small and far away. "I heard about your dad."

I swallow. My throat feels raw. "Yeah."

"I'm so sorry," she says. "Are you okay?"

The word okay feels like a joke. My father's dead. My mother sent me packing back to school early. I couldn't face seeing Vanessa anyway.

"I don't want to talk about it."

"I get that," she says softly. "But maybe you should. I mean, after everything he—"

"Don't." The word comes out sharp, cutting through the static. "Don't start."

"What I mean is—"

"I said don't!" I'm shouting now, and I can hear my own voice shake. "You didn't know him, okay? You didn't know what it was like."

"You told me what it was like," she whispers. "You told me everything."

"I didn't tell you everything." The room feels smaller, the air thicker. "And it's none of your business." I say it to hurt her. And I feel the hurt through the phone—I hear it in the way she pauses, hesitating. Caught on 'everything.' Because we were best

friends. We always promised to tell each other everything. Always. But I've admitted I've spent years hiding things.

"I'm your best friend," she says. "It is my business."

"Well, you shouldn't be," I snap. "You shouldn't care."

Another pause, but then, quietly: "You don't mean that."

"Don't tell me what I mean." My hands are shaking now. "Just—don't call me again, okay? I don't need this."

"Wait—"

But I ended the call. The silence that follows is worse than the shouting. I stare at the phone until the screen goes dark. And then I block her number.

That's the last time we ever spoke.

Or at least, that's what I remembered. But now, in this dream, it feels like I'm remembering it for the first time.

The guilt hits like a wave. My chest tightens. I never said goodbye. Not to my mom, not to Vanessa, not to my father.

The darkness around me begins to shift again—pulling me upward through deep water. I feel weightless. My heartbeat sounds slow and far away.

Another flash—

I'm little again. I can't be more than nine or ten. I'm standing in the hallway of my old house again. It's night. The air smells of whiskey and sweat and burnt food. I can hear him yelling from the kitchen. My mother's voice—pleading, breaking.

I want to turn away, but I can't. I'm frozen, watching through the doorway as he throws a bottle against the wall. It shatters near her shoulder. She screams. He grabs her wrist, pulls her close, spits out words I can't understand.

I want to run in, to stop him, to do something. But all I can do is stand there, my hands trembling.

And then—he looks up. Right at me. His eyes meet mine,

full of emotions I can't name. Not simply anger—more. Regret? Shame? Fear?

He lets go of her. He steps back. And then he leaves. A door slams.

My mother sinks to the floor, sobbing. I kneel beside her, and she whispers, "It's okay. It's okay, baby."

But it's not. It hasn't been for a long time, and it never will be again.

The darkness peeled away like layers. Gray at first, then lighter, until it bled away into reality. I was awake again, laying back on the couch, that little slip of paper on the floor next to my feet.

All these years, and I had forgotten I'd blocked Vanessa's number. I'd always wondered why she'd never called again, but my pride wouldn't let me reach out.

The one time, the following summer when I'd sent her a text message. A simple *hey*. It had gone unanswered.

CHAPTER TWENTY-NINE

I DIDN'T SLEEP well that night. Every time I rolled over, I could swear I'd heard a sound—one that didn't belong in the house. The windows rattled, slightly, as if the night winds were testing their strength. A faint scratching at the roof, too slow and deliberate to be a tree branch. And beneath it all, under the hum of my thoughts, I could have sworn I heard a whisper—soft, distant, at the top of the stair landing. It was almost as if someone, or something, was trying to send me a message.

The house—alive again. I could almost feel it breathing.

I tried to convince myself it was imagination, a trick of exhaustion, but it was a weak lie. There was a pulse in the walls—like the old bones of the place remembered what I didn't want to. Every creak of the floorboards beneath my bed, every sigh of air through the vents, felt intentional. I didn't feel like myself anymore. I felt like eighteen-year-old Grace again—the girl who was told never to come back here.

All of my old fears had reawakened. The fear that any

minute my father would come thundering into the house, drunk and angry.

I sat up in bed, pulling the blanket around my shoulders, my eyes straining in the dark. The faint moonlight painted bars across the wall, like a cage. My phone screen glowed on the nightstand. 2:47 a.m.

I should have turned on the light. I should have turned on the TV, or at least pretended everything was fine. But I couldn't move. It wasn't fear—it was heavier, thicker. Thick dread that settled deep in your stomach and wouldn't let you breathe deeply.

The whisper came again, clearer this time. A single word—though I couldn't make it out. It could have been my name, or it could have been the wind dragging through the attic vents. Either way, it sent a tremor through me. I held my breath, listening. The house answered back with silence.

I swung my legs over the edge of the bed. The floorboards were cold under my feet, colder than they should've been. I hadn't turned the heat off, but it felt like standing barefoot on ice. I glanced at the door—half-open, the same as I'd left it—and for a moment, I thought I saw a shadow move on the other side. Not walking. Shifting, like someone standing still but breathing.

My throat squeezed in on itself.

When I finally forced myself to step forward, the boards groaned under my weight. "Hello?" My voice came out softer than I meant it to, almost a whisper itself. No response. Nothing but the faint ticking of the heater vent.

I should have gone back to bed and pretended I wasn't terrified.

But I didn't.

Creeping out onto the landing, I blinked, trying to see clearly in the dark.

The staircase looked darker than usual, the shadows pooling thickly between the steps. I flicked on the hallway light, but it only hummed and flickered once before dying out completely. Perfect.

I reached for the banister, the wood smooth and familiar beneath my palm, though it was faintly damp. The air smelled different now—stale, like wet leaves and rust.

The whisper again. Clearer this time. "Grace."

A chill ran up my spine, goosebumps racing down my arms, the little hairs popping upright.

"Who's there?" I asked.

I leaned against the wall, trying to calm down, but my hands wouldn't stop trembling. I looked toward the bedroom door. It was still open. And for a moment, I thought I saw a shadow shift inside.

And then nothing. No whispers. No weird shadows. Reaching into the bedroom, I flicked on the light switch. It came on right away, the brightness blinding me for a moment. Where I'd thought I'd seen a shadow, were just my sheer curtains, hanging limp on the side of the window.

When I finally crawled back into bed, I kept the bedside lamp on. I didn't close my eyes for the rest of the night. Because I believed, deep down, I hadn't been imagining things.

The house… or a spirit here in the house… wanted me to remember.

MAY 2, 2009

I don't even know where to start tonight. My hands are still shaking as I write this. The house is finally quiet and yet my mind won't stop spinning. I can hear the echo of his voice in every corner, that deep, sharp tone that makes both me and her freeze in place. I used to know the man behind it. I don't anymore.

He wasn't always this way. I think back to when she was little—when he would laugh so hard that our Gracie would giggle just because she loved the sound of it. He used to kiss her on the top of her head when he tucked her in. Now, she flinches when he walks into the room. I see it. She tries to hide it, to be brave for me, but I know that look. It's the same one I wear when I catch myself holding my breath, waiting to see what version of him is coming through the door tonight.

I keep telling myself I can handle it, that I can protect her. But lately, I'm not so sure. He's angrier now. The smallest things set him off. Tonight it was the dishes. She forgot to wash one plate, and before I could step in, his rage flared up. I can see her shrinking. A smaller version of the bold Grace she's always been. She's in those delicate teenage years. And she should have her daddy on her side. It's heartbreaking. And so much of it is my fault.

Why did I stay so long? Why do I still stay? I'm scared that if I don't, he'll fight for custody. And then she'll be left alone with him.

Or worse, that a divorce would set him off and be the thing that makes him snap.

I want to take her and run. I think about it every night. I even keep a small bag packed in the back of the closet. Just in case. But where would we go? How would I keep her safe? He watches everything now. My phone, the car mileage, even the grocery receipts. I feel trapped, but I can't let that stop me. I have to find a way out before something happens that we can't take back.

I have to find a way. Or one day me or Grace won't be here. We won't survive one of his… explosions.

CHAPTER THIRTY

I'D BEEN READING my mom's old journal entries—flipping through them until something that seemed important caught my eye. The older ones crumbled at the edges, the newer ones written in a steadier hand. There was no order to my searching, no real plan. I was led by the pull of curiosity and a force I couldn't explain. Each entry felt like a doorway half-open, a glimpse into her thoughts that never let me in all the way. Her handwriting looped and swayed, hurried, while in other places it was deliberate, as if she were trying to pin down emotions.

As I read, a strange thing tickled the back of my mind. Certain phrases, certain turns of thought, felt too close, too known. I could almost hear her voice speaking through the pages, not the voice I remembered, but one older, wiser, or perhaps more tired. It was as though she had been writing directly to me, though that couldn't be true. Still, a thought tugged at the edge of my mind, like a word I couldn't recall or a dream I'd forgotten upon waking.

The more I read, the stronger the feeling grew—it was

as if an important bit of information was hovering beyond reach. It was unsettling. I struggled to make sense of it, looking for a hidden pattern to reveal everything. Each page brought me closer to knowing—it was there, waiting. I was standing on the edge of a memory that wasn't mine. My mind was grappling with the truth that had been quietly shaping me all along.

I knew what could have happened, but I also didn't want to let my brain go there. But pieces of the puzzle floated around me. *My father's body, never recovered.* I still couldn't understand how I'd never know this. *My mom, obsessed with protecting me.* This part wasn't shocking at all. She'd always been that way. *Aunt Clara losing her mind.* This part was weird, but it had to be connected. She must know something. Whatever happened, she knew—maybe it had sent her over the edge.

My mom telling me not to come home. That part was harder. Maybe she couldn't face me after everything. Maybe she was afraid I would find out the truth.

I flipped through her journals, searching for hints. There were dozens and dozens of entries of her being worried about protecting me. I could see how my father's anger built through the years.

At the time, I hadn't seen it that way—it was always scary to me, and I probably became desensitized as I got older. So the anger was getting worse, but it always felt bad to me.

But reading my mother's journals, I could see how his fuse got shorter and the rage got bigger. I shook as I read a few of those entries, the tears falling as my stomach clenched in on itself. My mother's fear in those entries was palpable. And beyond fear—a desperation so thick it grew into an insatiable hunger for freedom. For escape.

My mother had been cheating… and there was a good possibility her lover killed my father and made it look like an accident. Had my mother known? Or worse… Did she help Phillip cover it up?

Oh Mom. What did you do?

APRIL 20, 2012

I miss my Gracie so much. I told her not to come home again. It was the hardest letter I ever had to write. I know she doesn't understand why I'm pushing her away. Maybe that's for the best.

The house is too full of ghosts. Every floorboard remembers. The stain on the carpet—I thought I got it all out, but sometimes, when the light hits just right, I swear I still see it. Maybe that's only in my head. I scrubbed until my hands bled, and still it lingers.

She's called so many times. Left voicemails and texted. I can hear the desperation in her voice. It kills me not to answer. Not to call my baby girl back and comfort her. But what good could come of that? She can't come back here…

If she comes back, it might all come rushing back too. The shouting. The crash. The stillness afterward. She's fragile, and I can't risk breaking her again. To remember would be the worst possible thing for her. Then she would have to live with the knowledge.

I'll carry this myself, and I'll keep carrying it. If that's the price of her peace, then so be it. Let her think I'm mad at her—better than her knowing the truth. As long as she never remembers… as long as she never remembers.

CHAPTER THIRTY-ONE

I NEEDED answers and there was no one left to ask except Aunt Clara. Although I realized it might be futile, I had to try. So after spending the day catching up on work, I headed back to the nursing home.

The smell hit me again the second I stepped into the nursing home—sterile, like bleach mixed with a sourish odor.

I signed in at the front desk. The receptionist recognized me, smiled too brightly, and waved me through. Aunt Clara must be doing good since I didn't have to wait for the nurse to escort me.

I wondered what they saw when I visited—the dutiful niece clinging to the last branch of the family, or the idiot who kept coming back, expecting a coherent conversation with a patient who was already half gone.

A nurse at the desk spotted me lingering and smiled politely. I vaguely remembered her from my last visit but hadn't caught her name. "Clara's in her room, but she's up and working on a puzzle." I nodded and turned toward Aunt Clara's door, which hung half-open.

Pushing it all the way, I found her sitting in her chair with a small folding table set up in front of her. She had a puzzle mostly completed.

"Aunt Clara," I said, trying to sound cheerful.

She looked up, squinted, and the confusion passed through her eyes like a cloud shadowing the sun. "You came back," she finally said. "You shouldn't have."

I froze, then forced a smile. "I wanted to see you."

Her mouth folded into what could be a frown or a grimace. "You shouldn't be here," she repeated, quieter this time. "It's not safe."

Safe. She said it like she was warning a child about a busy street.

I sat in the small chair across from her. "I wanted to ask you a question. About Mom."

She'd already turned back to the puzzle, her gnarled fingers sifting through pieces. "You have to water in the mornings," she muttered. "Not in the afternoon. The sun burns the leaves." Gardening advice.

I watched her work. Her hands trembled but were still graceful in their own way.

I opened my mouth. "Aunt Clara… Why did you and Mom start fighting?"

She hummed to herself. A faint tune, old and broken. I thought it might be "You Are My Sunshine."

"You used to be close, I swear I never even heard you argue when I was a kid," I pressed. "I want to know what happened. I have been reading her journal, and… and I read your journal too."

That got a reaction. Her hand froze mid-motion. Slowly, she lifted her head and turned toward me. "You shouldn't have done that."

"I needed to understand."

"You shouldn't have read it." Barely a whisper.

"What secret were you talking about?" My voice cracked. "What were you hiding?"

Her breathing hitched. "Some things stay buried," she whispers. "Heidi knew that."

"Mom?" My heart pounded. "What did she know?"

But she was already drifting again, eyes on the puzzle in front of her. "These begonias are too close together," she murmured. "They'll choke each other if you're not careful."

"Aunt Clara, please." I tried to keep the frustration out of my voice. "I know something happened between you and Mom. And I think it has to do with my father."

Her lips twisted. "The garden."

"Yes." I exhaled slowly. "What happened?"

She looked at her hands, but it seemed like she was looking through them—like she could see something I couldn't. "Heidi wanted to dig deeper," she said softly. "She shouldn't have. It was already—" She stopped, pressing her fingers to her mouth. "No. No, that's not right."

"What was already what?" I asked.

Her gaze snapped up to me. "You shouldn't be back here."

The way she said it made the hair rise on my arms. There was a rawness in her tone—fear, maybe. Or guilt. But I didn't know if she meant there at White Oak or here in Bleeding Hearts Valley.

I leaned closer. "Back where?" I said it gently, but I needed to know what she meant.

Her eyes darted to the window, and she focused on whatever she saw out there. Her window overlooked the garden. Her eyes were locked on the view. They darted back to me, and then back to the garden.

"Here?" I whispered. "You mean the garden?"

She shook her head. "The other one."

My pulse quickened. "Mom's garden?"

She didn't answer. Instead, she hummed again, the same broken tune. Her fingers picked at the hem of her cardigan.

I stared out the window, watching the small tree in the middle of their small garden. The leaves danced in the breeze.

When I looked back, Aunt Clara was staring at it too. "She planted a similar tree," she murmurs. "Said it reminded her of family." She was talking about the crab apple tree my mother planted in the backyard.

"What did it remind her of?"

"She never told me." Her gaze shifted, distant now. "She said it had to stay there. To keep it quiet."

My stomach dropped. "Keep what quiet?"

Her hands started to shake. "You look like her," she said. "When you frown."

"Aunt Clara, please." I was feeling desperate by then. "What was Mom keeping quiet? What were you both hiding?"

But she was gone again, her attention swallowed. "You have to pull the weeds before they take over," she murmured. "They'll strangle everything if you let them."

I closed my eyes, trying not to scream.

The nurse poked her head in the door. "Everything okay in here?"

"Yeah," I lied. "We're fine."

She nodded and disappeared back into the hallway. I

turned back to Clara. "I read your journal. About what you wrote—'Don't tell.' Don't tell what?"

She paused. Her hands hovered over the puzzle, placing a piece in and tapping it down. "Heidi wanted to protect you."

"From what?"

Her lips moved, forming silent words. Then she said, almost to herself, "From what she did."

The words landed like a weight in my gut. The room spun around me. "What did she do?"

Aunt Clara looked at me—really looked this time. There was a sharpness in her gaze, a flash of lucidity that was terrifying in its clarity. "You shouldn't dig," she whispered.

A chill ran down my spine. "Dig what?" My voice was so low, I couldn't believe she even heard me.

Her mouth twitched. "The tree knows."

"The crab apple tree?"

She nodded faintly. "That's where she buried it."

"Buried what?" My voice was still barely a whisper.

But the moment was gone. Her gaze drifted, eyes glassy again. "The soil's too dry," she said absently. "Needs water."

I sat there for a long time, watching her sort through the pieces, feeling the questions piling up like stones in my chest.

After a while, she started telling a story about a garden party that probably never happened. I let her talk. Maybe the truth was buried in the babble.

"She wore a yellow dress," Aunt Clara said dreamily. "Said it was her lucky one. The neighbors brought pie. Everyone said how beautiful the garden looked. No one knew then." This must be a fantasy of Aunt Clara's because Dotty specifically said my mother kept to herself. I couldn't imagine she was having parties in the garden with the neighbors.

"Knew what?" I asked faintly, my mind elsewhere.

"It was underneath them all along."

The words made my throat go dry. "What was underneath them?"

She smiled faintly. "The truth."

The nurse returned to tell me visiting hours were over. I nodded numbly, standing up. Aunt Clara didn't seem to notice me leaving.

The drive home felt longer than usual. The sky hung low and gray, threatening rain. I kept replaying her words—*the tree knows… that's where she buried it.* Buried what? Something my mother did? Whatever it was, did Aunt Clara help her?

When I pulled into my driveway, instead of walking up the steps to the front door, I walked around the side of the yard, opening the gate to the backyard and slipping through.

The garden loomed before me. Mom's garden. The one she was so obsessed with before she died. The crab apple tree stood near the back door, gnarled and dark against the fading light.

My heart thudded, making my chest visibly rise with each beat. Every instinct told me to leave it alone. To let the past rot quietly where it was. But then I thought of the journals and what Aunt Clara had said.

I walked over to the tree. The grass was wet underfoot, the air sharp with the scent of earth and decaying leaves.

The crab apple tree looked worse up close—bark split, branches knotted like veins. The ground beneath it was uneven, softer than the rest of the yard. I knelt down and pressed my palm against the soil. Cold seeped through my skin.

Aunt Clara's words played through my head. *She buried it.* A shiver ran through me. For a second, I imagined I could feel the ground pulsing faintly below—like a heartbeat deep in the dirt. I jerked back, almost falling on my ass.

I went inside through the back door. Inside, the house was too quiet. I flicked on a light and started a pot of coffee. I was the deep kind of cold that needed warming inside and out.

A knock at the window jolted me. I spun, heart hammering—but it was a branch scraping the glass. I exhaled shakily.

Hot cup of coffee in hand, and a blanket wrapped around me, I went upstairs and curled up in my bed, grabbing one of the journals I'd left on my nightstand. I needed to keep reading to find answers.

JUNE 1, 2026

So much time has passed since I last saw my sweet girl's face. I miss her warm hugs, the little high pitch squeal of her laughter. I miss every single thing about her.

Every day I think about reaching out to her but I know I can't. There's too much at risk. She can't know the truth. It's better this way. She can move on from this life.

I failed at protecting her from her father. I should have gotten us out years ago. For her to have dealt with him all those years in her childhood. I should have taken her and left. But I didn't. And things got worse and worse. I was no longer safe, and neither was she.

But now she can go on and live her life not having to know —it's a weight she shouldn't have to bear. That's on me.

I'm so sorry my sister had to help me. And that she had to know the truth. She's always been the strong one and I don't understand why she's collapsed under the weight of this secret.

CHAPTER THIRTY-TWO

I DREAMED about my father again that night. Having fallen asleep with my mother's journal open on my chest, my mind racing with possibilities, it was no surprise the direction my dreams took.

In my dream, he was sitting at the kitchen table. The light above him hummed and flickered, turning his face into a stop-motion of anger and tenderness. He was drinking straight from a bottle of whiskey—and every time he set it down, the sound echoed, hollow and wet. There was rain against the window. Heavy. Relentless. His swallows were deep and audible.

He looked at me, eyes glassy, and said, "You shouldn't have seen that."

When I tried to answer, mud seeped up from the kitchen tiles, thick and dark. His hand slid across the table toward me, but it wasn't not a hand anymore—it was a clump of wet earth, worms writhing through it. His voice dropped lower, almost gentle. "She did this."

I woke up gasping.

My mouth tasted earthy. The sheets were twisted

around my legs, damp with sweat, and for a few seconds I could still smell the rain from the dream—heavy, electric.

It was five in the morning.

I told myself it was a dream, my brain chewing on old ghosts, but it felt different this time. The words he said—*She did this*—wouldn't leave my head.

I got up, pulled on a sweatshirt, and padded out onto the landing. The house creaked in familiar places, but it felt foreign tonight, like an intruder rearranged it in my sleep.

I walked downstairs slowly, without a real plan.

The moonlight slanted through the window above the kitchen sink, pooling over the counter, the tile, the same spot where—

No.

I pressed my palms to the cool surface, trying to breathe past the rising bile in my throat. The dream's residue lingered like static. Dad's voice, the mud, the rain. And suddenly, I remembered a detail I shouldn't.

Her shovel.

I made coffee and scrolled through my phone, letting the noise fill the room. By the time I was pouring myself a cup, I had convinced myself I was losing it.

The rest of the day drifted by in fog. I kept catching flashes. Thunder, glass breaking, my mother's voice shouting my name. When the rain started that evening—soft at first, then steadier—I felt my pulse sync with it.

The sun was already setting when I finally opened the back door and stepped outside.

The backyard was slick with mud. The air smelled like old leaves and rust. I stood near the tree, staring at the patch of ground that didn't look right. Softer, darker, a subtle dip in the earth with more weeds than the other grassy areas.

I knelt down, feeling the wetness soak through my sweatpants.

And just like that, I cracked open inside.

The memory didn't return all at once. It came in pieces, sharp and disjointed.

I'm younger. Barefoot. Standing in the rain. The water's up to my ankles. I'm shivering, holding a heavy object—a flashlight, I think. Mom's voice is shaking. "Go inside, sweetheart. Please."

But I don't move. I stand and watch her. She's digging. Each shovel sinks into the mud with a sick, wet sound.

Behind her, through the open door, the kitchen light flickers. And there—barely visible through the doorway—is my father.

He's lying on the floor. His arm bent at an impossible angle. There's blood—dark and spreading—reflecting the light like oil.

Behind him, Aunt Clara is frantically moving around the room. Doing who knows what. She looks like a chicken with her head cut off.

I drop the flashlight, and the beam lands on his face. Eyes open. Unseeing.

I stumbled backward now, in the present, falling into the mud. The rain was cold against my skin, but my body was burning.

Mom's voice echoed through time. *He can't hurt us again. It's okay. Everything's okay. I promise.*

I covered my ears, but the words wouldn't stop.

Thirteen years of silence, of pretending he vanished. Thirteen years of ignoring the gaps in my memory.

But I remembered now.

The rain. The mud. The shovel. Mom digging.

And me, standing there watching.

The rain pounded harder now, drumming against my hood, soaking through my clothes. The memory swirled in my mind, looping over and over—the wet shovel, the hollowed ground, the flash of his eyes in the kitchen light. I felt like a teenager again, naive and helpless, only this time there was no one to guide me, no one to tell me it was over.

I remembered her face one last time, thirteen years ago, pressed tight in anguish as she shoveled. But now there was no one. No explanation, no apology, no guidance. I was left with the weight of what she did and the knowledge that I saw it all, even if I had tried to forget.

I knelt there on the ground for what felt like hours. The rain soaked my clothes completely.

Eventually, I pushed myself to my feet. I was dripping wet, mud caking my fingers and knees. I glanced back at the house—the place that once felt safe, it harbored so many secrets—and I felt the first sharp slice of grief. Not so much for him, but for her, for the version of my life that could have been.

I knew I couldn't unsee everything. I couldn't undo it. And I couldn't run from it. I swallowed the lump in my throat, bit back a scream, and for the first time in thirteen years, I faced it fully.

Some things would never wash away.

Some things lay buried, and yet, they always found a way to surface.

WELLINGS HARDWARE

- - - - - - - - - - - - - - - - - -

2XMTL SHOVEL....................36.88
10LB ORG FRTLZR............. 27.99

- - - - - - - - - - - - - - - - - -

TOTAL:

CHAPTER THIRTY-THREE

THE NEXT MORNING, a sharp knock at the door startled me while I was sitting in the kitchen sipping my coffee and scrolling through my work emails. I went to the front door and paused. I needed to install a doorbell camera, obviously. Sighing, I unlocked the door and swung it open.

Vanessa was standing on the front porch with a container.

"Hey! I hope it's not too weird to randomly drop by, but I was over at my parents' house and my mom made these cinnamon rolls. I figured I'd drop off a couple for you." The scent of the rolls was clinging to her, she didn't even need to open the lid.

"Oh… that sounds great. I'm getting caught up on work emails, but do you want to come in for a minute?" I asked, gesturing behind me. She hesitated and then shrugged.

"Sure, I have a few minutes. I have work to do today too. I can start later, but I'd love to chat!" She walked into the house past me. A truck at the end of the driveway had slowed down almost to a stop, and I recognised it immediately.

Thomas.

What the fuck was he doing?

I stood in the doorway and made sure he saw me flip him off. He stepped on the gas and peeled off in a hurry.

"What was that all about?" Vanessa asked from behind me and I closed and locked the door, turning back to her.

"Come have a cup of coffee." I laughed, shaking my head. But even I recognized how hollow the laugh sounded.

In the kitchen, she opened the cinnamon rolls and the steam released a heavy scent, making my mouth water. I poured myself a second cup of coffee and pulled down a mug for her. Once we were seated, I waited until I'd had a bite of the roll, savoring the gooey sweetness before answering her question.

"Thomas Andrews. He's a realtor who has been harassing me."

"Harassing you?"

"Yeah, he's dead set on me selling this place to a developer. I don't know, I told him I wasn't interested and to fuck off, basically."

She laughed for a minute and then her face got serious again.

"So are you thinking of staying then?"

I paused. The answer was right there on my tongue, but I wasn't ready to make it official. "I'm thinking about it. Maybe." I shrugged again. She was looking over my shoulder and I turned my head. The window was right behind me with a perfect overview of Mom's garden. A shiver ran down my back.

"I don't remember your backyard being this… landscaped?" Even though a lot of the plants were bare right now, due to the changing season, it was evident it was a well-planned garden. She stood and walked to the window. The way she was inspecting it made me nervous, as though she knew secrets even I hadn't deciphered, although that couldn't be possible. Could it?

"When did your mother do all this? And the tree... you didn't have an apple tree in your backyard?"

"Apparently after I headed to college, Mom decided to take up gardening. According to my neighbor, she was very serious about it."

"Wow. That's... so random." She laughed for a minute but she was still staring out the window, almost like she could see what I had remembered. The room suddenly went very cold, and the hairs on the back of my neck stood on end. I could feel goosebumps traveling down my arms.

"Well, it was so nice of you to drop by with these rolls—please let your mother know they are still the best on the block! I do need to get back to work, though." I waved my hand toward my laptop.

She slowly turned back to me, like she was reluctant to leave the window.

"Yeah, I should be going anyway. Thanks for the coffee! Maybe we can get together again soon? It was so nice hanging out with you..."

"Yeah, maybe." I wanted to say no, but I couldn't think of a good reason to. It *had* been nice seeing her again. But why was she being so nosy about the garden?

I walked her to the door and when she was gone, I locked it and went back to my laptop. Before I went back to my work emails, I clicked on the search browser and typed a name.

I stared at the search bar, the name *Thomas Andrews*

blinking back at me like a challenge. Realtor, was the title on his card—*Andrews Realty Group* in embossed silver letters—but I needed to know more about this guy. What started as an annoying nuisance was taking a different turn.

My fingers hovered over the keyboard for a moment before I hit Enter. Pages loaded—slowly, like the internet itself didn't want me to see.

The first few hits were predictable. Listings for mid-tier condos, smiling headshots, boilerplate lines about his 'local expertise.' His website looked polished, generic, sterile. You could swap out his photo with anyone in a suit and no one would notice.

But that was what bothered me. *No edges.* Too sterile. Too… calculated. I dug deeper. LinkedIn, Facebook, the usual digital graveyards. His LinkedIn had exactly one connection—Andrews Realty Group—and even that appeared fake, like a placeholder. Facebook was even thinner, a single photo of a sunset and nothing else. No comments, no likes, no friends.

A realtor with no social footprint? Impossible. Realtors lived online. They thrived on visibility.

My pulse quickened.

I tried a new search. *Thomas Andrews developer deal.*

That's when the tone changed.

There were a few scattered mentions—articles from business journals, obscure PDFs from city council minutes. Andrews' name tucked in the middle of paragraphs, like an afterthought. Always adjacent to a larger entity. *Kerrigan Development Group, Danton Real Estate Holdings, Summit Ventures.* Big names. Bigger money. Deals big enough to reshape neighborhoods.

In one article from three years ago, he was quoted

about "community revitalization." His smile in the accompanying photo didn't reach his eyes.

Then nothing for six months. No new listings, no news, no social updates.

Until last month—one brief mention on a property blog. A minor note. "Local realtor Thomas Andrews assisted in brokering the purchase of the old Tanner Industrial lot."

I leaned back, scrolling, trying to piece him together. My coffee had gone cold.

The silence in the room pressed in. I thought about the two men I'd seen outside the previous week. The image replayed now as I looked through the empty pages of his life. Trying to fit these clues together.

I tried a reverse image search on his headshot. No matches. Not one. Even the metadata on the photo file from his website had been scrubbed clean.

The unease shifted, turning colder. What I'd thought was a desperate pushy realtor… might be much worse.

I clicked deeper into the city's public records. Property transfers, tax filings, permit applications. Andrews' name surfaced again, but always inconsistently spelled—Tom A. Andrews, T. L. Andrews, even "Andrews, Consultant." As if he were hiding in the paperwork.

One entry caught my eye: a development proposal for a warehouse conversion signed by *Summit Ventures*, listing Andrews as "liaison." The project had been "deferred indefinitely." Could that be the issue the two goons had confronted him about in front of my driveway?

Deferred. A bureaucratic euphemism for *'something went wrong.'*

I copied the file name, cross-checked it with the council archive, and found a footnote I almost missed: "Conflict of interest investigation pending." Thomas' name was underlined in red.

I sat there, staring at it, heart drumming in my ears.

Whatever Thomas Andrews was involved in, it wasn't real estate. And whatever those two goons had said to him outside… they weren't giving him a casual warning.

I continued to scroll and found only one mention of him in anything hinting at any semblance of a personal life. The briefest mention of him. An obituary with a name that sent off alarm bells. A familiar name.

Obituary: Detective Phillip Andrews (1958–2018)

Detective Phillip James Andrews, a devoted father, respected investigator, and longtime member of the Bleeding Hearts Valley community, perished in a car accident on October 12, 2018, at the age of 60.

Born and raised in Bleeding Hearts Valley, Phillip dedicated four decades of his life to the pursuit of truth and justice. From his earliest days on the force, he was known for his calm presence, tireless work ethic, and unwavering belief that every case—no matter how small—deserved to be solved. His colleagues often said he had a way of listening that made people tell him what they hadn't meant to.

Detective Andrews joined the Bleeding Hearts Valley Police Department in 1981 and served with distinction. Over the course of his career, he investigated many of the town's most complex and emotionally charged cases, always with compassion for victims and an unshakable sense of duty.

Though he received numerous commendations, Phillip never sought recognition. He believed the real reward was in restoring peace to the people who had lost it. His friends recall that even on the toughest nights, when an investigation seemed to reach a dead end, he would say softly, "There's always something left to find."

Outside the badge, Phillip was a quiet man who loved long drives through the valley's back roads, and strong coffee at dawn. Those who knew him best remember his dry humor, his deep sense of empathy, and his quiet strength in the face of hardship.

Detective Andrews leaves behind his beloved son, Thomas Andrews; his sister, Margaret Holt of Crescent Hill; and a community forever marked by his integrity and kindness.

A memorial service will be held at Bleeding Hearts Valley Community Church on October 20, 2018, at 2:00 p.m., followed by a gathering at the Veterans Hall. In lieu of flowers, the family asks that donations be made to the Bleeding Hearts Valley Youth Center or the Cold Case Victims' Fund, two causes close to Phillip's heart.

Detective Phillip Andrews will be remembered not only for the cases he solved, but for the quiet dignity with which he lived his life—a man who believed in truth, in justice, and in the idea that no one, living or lost, should ever be forgotten.

CHAPTER THIRTY-FOUR

SO THOMAS' father was a detective. *It's always the preacher's daughter, the cop's son, isn't it?* It seemed so cliche. I type the father's name in the search bar. An article popped up about the car accident he died in. Lots of articles about his contributions to the community, investigations he was involved in.

And then there was an article about his investigation into my father's death. Several articles. Apparently he was in charge of the investigation. There were a lot of duplicate articles to the ones I'd seen at the library, but I hadn't been paying attention to who was overseeing the investigation. Why would I? I didn't think it was relevant. But was there a link?

Knowing it was Thomas' father raised the hair on my arms. I didn't believe in coincidences. There was a reason Thomas was coming around and being so pushy.

Reading the article, I paused. My father had been at the bar that night? Of course he had…

Bleeding Hearts Chronicle

Search for Missing Local Man Concludes—Authorities Rule Patrick Jenkins Presumed Dead

January 19, 2012 – Bleeding Hearts Valley

BLEEDING HEARTS — After nearly two months of investigation, authorities have officially closed the case of missing resident Patrick Jenkins, who vanished in late November under what police now describe as "tragic accidental circumstances."

According to the Bleeding Hearts County Sheriff's Department, Jenkins' pickup truck was recovered from the depths of Moon Lake, a notoriously murky body of water known for its steep drop-offs and unpredictable currents.

Although Jenkins' body was not recovered, investigators believe he perished when his truck veered off the embankment during a late-night drive.

"Given the evidence—the position of the vehicle, the personal effects recovered inside, and the absence of any indication of foul play—we're confident this was a tragic accident," said Detective Phillip Andrews, who led the investigation. "Moon Lake has claimed lives before. The depth and cold make recovery extremely difficult. Sadly, it's not uncommon for remains to never surface."

Family and friends of Jenkins, had held out hope he might still be found alive after he was last seen leaving McCready's Bar on the evening of November 26.

Authorities said weather conditions at the time of the accident—heavy rain and limited visibility—may have contributed to Jenkins' apparent loss of control.

Detective Andrews confirmed the case is now officially closed, pending any new evidence.

"Our hearts go out to the Jenkins family," Andrews added. "It's always painful when there are no remains to lay to rest, but the investigation has reached its end. We're confident in our findings."

A small vigil is planned for next weekend at the Moon Lake overlook to honor Patrick Jenkins' memory.

CHAPTER THIRTY-FIVE

THE BACK of my mind was still gnawing at me, a bit of truth—just out of reach—a shadow of an idea, an answer I could almost touch but couldn't quite hold. It was Thomas. Or maybe it was his father. I couldn't separate the two anymore. Every time I started to piece it together, the image slipped sideways, like when you wake up from a dream and you can remember the edges of it.

I kept telling myself I was overthinking it. But then I saw the way Thomas looked at me now—measured, careful, like he was waiting for me to reveal a weakness. Maybe he already knew I was onto him. Or maybe he was as lost as I was, caught in the same web of half-truths and old ghosts.

Still… There was something about his father I couldn't shake.

Last night I found an old clipping in one of my mother's boxes—Thomas's father in the paper, smiling beside the mayor at a charity event. I knew it was no coincidence. It was dated before my father's accident, so it wasn't like my mother started following him afterwards.

I'd been avoiding going outside. I'd been sleeping on the couch, if you can call it that—half-awake, half-watching the window for shadows moving when they shouldn't. That was where I was curled up when there was a knock at the door. I glanced at my phone—10AM. Not as early as I'd thought.

They knocked softly, two taps and a pause, like a heartbeat.

I almost didn't answer, but whoever it was would probably stand there until I did. So I opened the door.

"Good morning, dear," Dotty said, smiling, holding a casserole dish like an offering. "You've been worrying yourself to the bone, I can tell. You're looking thin."

I forced a smile, though I hadn't looked in a mirror all day. "Thanks, Dotty. You don't have to keep doing this."

"Oh, nonsense." She brushed past me before I could protest, setting the dish on the kitchen counter. "It's no trouble. Besides, I like to check in. It's what neighbors do. And I'm glad to see you got those steps fixed!"

Dotty wandered over to the window above the sink, peering out toward the backyard. "Your mother's garden is still holding up," she said, her tone drifting toward nostalgia. "Even after all these years, and this chilly fall—all this rain... She had such a green thumb, didn't she?"

"Yeah," I said softly. "I guess she did."

Dotty glanced at me, her eyes narrowing slightly, like she was trying to decide how much to say. "She used to spend hours out there," she said. "Even when the weather turned. I'd see her from my kitchen window, digging and digging. There were times I thought she'd go right through to the other side of the world."

She chuckled lightly, but her smile didn't reach her eyes.

"What was she planting?" I asked before I could stop myself.

"Oh, I couldn't say. Herbs, bulbs, or weeds she said were too stubborn to pull." Dotty gave a little shrug, but her expression flickered—a hesitation, *a decision not to say more.*

When I didn't answer, she looked around the kitchen, her gaze falling on the stack of journals on the table. "What's that?"

I moved instinctively, like I needed to protect the journals. Scooting them closer to me. She wouldn't open one, would she? Well, I couldn't be sure.

"Oh, these are my mom's old journals. Nothing interesting." I shrugged.

She nodded slowly. "I recognize a few of them. Your mother had a lot on her mind those last few years. I'd come over for tea and she'd be writing even while we talked. Said she didn't want to forget things. I think maybe…"

She trailed off again, then smiled quickly. "Anyway, I'll let you get back to it. You don't forget to eat, all right? You look like you haven't slept in a week."

When the door shut behind her, I stood there for a long moment, staring out at the garden. The earth looked heavy, wet from last night's rain. It almost seemed to breathe.

And then I did what she told me to. Maybe because I missed having a mother telling me what to do. Maybe because I hadn't eaten since the morning before. Or maybe because having a little old lady bake me a french toast casserole made me feel safe.

I thought of Dotty's voice, soft and hesitant—*digging and digging*—and the thought made my stomach twist. Glancing out the window, I thought about how nice it would be to pour a patio back there right under the apple tree. I probably didn't have my mother's green thumb but I would have to learn how to maintain the backyard. So having a patio to sit out and enjoy it seemed like a good idea.

Looking down at the stack of journals, I admitted to myself, the journals were the only thing keeping me from completely unraveling.

While I ate, I flipped through one with entries written during the investigation into my father's accident. The tone seemed to shift as they progressed. The later entries were… colder. More detached. She wrote about *the investigation* in vague terms, about the "questions won't stop coming." About "the lies must stay buried."

Buried.

There was that word again.

Digging.

Buried.

Those two words seemed to keep coming up. Over and over again.

I flipped to one of the later volumes—brown leather, the edges stiff with age. The date at the top read December 14, 2011. My father had only been gone a couple of weeks.

I saw him again today. He shouldn't have come here. I told him we had to stop, we might get caught. If they find out, everything ends. Better to let this all fizzle out. Let it be buried with the rest of the… truth.

• • •

I closed the journal and pressed the heel of my hand against my eyes. My mind was spinning. What did she mean, *if they find out? Find out what?* I flipped ahead several pages, looking for any other clues. Then there was an entry in January, blotched with wet spots—definitely where tear stains spread the ink in little circles, making it harder to read. But a name on the page made my heart stop.

JANUARY 15, 2012

It's over. I am so heartbroken. I didn't think I could be any more heartbroken, but I have lost everything and there's no light at the end of the tunnel.

Yesterday we met for the final time. I wanted to stay in his arms forever. For a moment I wished I would die that way.

But after what he did for me—what he did to smooth things over and get the investigation closed—it was never going to be safe for us to have a public relationship. It would mar his reputation. And if anyone looked deeper... Well, who knows what could happen. So we ended it.

Truthfully, I could see the way he felt about me changed. And who could blame him? I don't look at myself the same way anymore either.

I keep replaying it in my mind, the way he wouldn't look at me when we said goodbye. Maybe he couldn't. Maybe it was easier for him to turn away than to look at me now—what we'd done to each other—what he'd done for me. I told myself he was protecting me, that he ended things because it was the safest and smartest thing to do. But now, in the silence, I can't stop wondering if it was another lie I wanted to believe.

There were moments when I thought he might change his mind. When his hand brushed mine and lingered a little too long, when his voice softened and I could almost see him saying we could make it work. I wanted to beg.

But I know that would be stupid and selfish.

I gave up Grace to protect her from the truth. And now I have to give up Phillip too.

I don't deserve him anyway. I don't deserve anything.

Phillip. It felt like my heart stopped for a minute. Phillip was the man who wrote the love letter. Phillip… was the man who my mother had an affair with—was in love with.

Phillip. Was Thomas' father. Detective Phillip Andrews. The same detective who investigated my father's accident.

Phillip closed the investigation to keep my mother from being caught.

Did Thomas know?

Who else in town might know? Who else might be digging for information?

I couldn't trust anyone.

CHAPTER THIRTY-SIX

I DIDN'T SLEEP WELL AGAIN. I was desperate for answers. To know the truth now. To have it confirmed. In the back of my mind, I felt like I knew.

I needed to see Aunt Clara again, and I needed a straight answer this time. Stepping into the nursing home again, that smell hit me in the face the second I opened the door. The receptionist barely glanced up this time. She gestured to the sign-in at the desk and waved me on.

I found Aunt Clara by the window, staring at the garden outside. The television was on, volume muted, an infomercial flickering. When she saw me, recognition passed through her eyes—for a moment—then vanished.

"Aunt Clara?" I said softly. "It's me. It's—"

"Gracie," she said suddenly. My name. Clear as day.

I froze. "Yes. It's me."

She blinked, lips twitching into a crooked smile. "You've grown into your mother's face."

I took the chair beside her and waited. On the way over, I'd rehearsed what I wanted to ask, but now I was sitting there, my throat tightened.

"You remember the house, right?" I began. "Mom's garden? The apple tree in the back?"

Aunt Clara's gaze drifted back to the window. "Too much shade for tomatoes," she murmured. As if that explained why my mother had chosen an apple tree instead.

"Yes." I leaned forward. "That's the one. She planted that tree after… after Dad died."

"Mmm." She stared out the window, humming softly to herself.

"Do you remember *why* she planted it? I found notes she wrote that made me wonder."

Aunt Clara's mouth worked silently for a few seconds before she spoke again. "Roots run deep. Deeper than you think."

"What does that mean?"

She laughed suddenly—a high, brittle sound that startled me.

"Patrick," she said, looking right at me.

My pulse thudded against my ribs.

"Patrick? What about him? What about my father?"

His name hung between us, heavy. She didn't respond.

After an eternity, Aunt Clara tilted her head, listening to sounds I couldn't hear. "It was so cold. He was so cold. So heavy. She said we had to."

My mouth went dry. I tried to swallow but my tongue was too thick for my mouth.

"Had to what?" I whispered. I could hear my own breathing, loud and shallow. I didn't wait for her answer. I knew. "You were there?" I knew the answer, but I asked anyway.

Her expression turned vacant again, the light gone.

"Birds in the branches," she mumbled. "Can't hear the worms underneath."

"Aunt Clara," I said, gripping the armrest to keep my hands steady. "Did she bury him under her tree?"

But she had turned away, humming again under her breath, eyes on the garden again. For a long minute, I sat there while the TV flickered onto a game show.

"Aunt Clara?" I tried again. Her eyes flicked to me quickly and then back to the TV. "I need to know. Whatever you tell me, I won't tell anyone," I croaked, my voice barely above a whisper. But I knew she heard me. Her shoulders tensed and she shifted in her chair. She turned to me and opened her mouth to speak.

The door pushed open just as Aunt Clara was about to say something, and she snapped her mouth shut, turning back to the TV.

The nurse who had pushed her way in announced it was dinner time. I wanted to ask more questions, but the nurse was already bustling Aunt Clara off to the dining room. She didn't even turn around to say goodbye, and I left, feeling defeated.

Outside, I sat in the car, gripping the steering wheel before leaving. I looked at myself in the rearview mirror. Aunt Clara was right—my face was my mother's.

The drive home blurred. I barely remember the turns, the stoplights. The steady echo of Aunt Clara's voice replayed over and over. *She said we had to.*

By the time I pulled into the driveway, the sun was already setting. The porch light flickered when I opened the door, as if the house itself recognized me, and wasn't sure it wanted to let me in.

The tree loomed in the backyard, its silhouette visible through the kitchen window. Even in the dark, I could make out its gnarled shape—thick trunk, low branches, roots that seemed to bulge against the ground like veins.

I couldn't stop thinking about what—or *who*—must be underneath it. My mind raced with Aunt Clara's words.

I found myself pulling out my laptop, fingers trembling as I typed into the search bar: how to build a backyard patio over tree roots.

The results were innocent enough—DIY home improvement blogs, YouTube tutorials—but all I saw were blueprints for concealment. Paving stones. Concrete slabs. Cover.

Covering it.

Covering *him*.

Covering for her.

If Mom had done it—if she'd killed him—it was for a good reason. To protect me. I remembered the fighting. The slammed doors. The smell of whiskey. Little bits from that night.

I was sure she had no choice.

I knew she must have saved me. And herself.

And now it was my turn to save *her*.

To keep the secret buried. To cover up her secret in a permanent way.

A to Z Patios & Decks LLC
123 Builder's Lane
Bleeding Hearts Valley, CA 95000
Email: info@atozpatios.com

INVOICE

Invoice #: 2024-1105-01

Bill To:
Grace Jenkins
518 Monmouth Drive
Bleeding Hearts Valley, CA 95000

Description of Work

	Description	QTY	Unit Price	AMT
1	Site Preparation (grading, form setup)	1 job	$350.00	$350.00
2	Concrete (4" thick, 4000 PSI, broom finish)	400 sq. ft.	$9.00 / sq. ft.	$3,600.00
3	Reinforcement (wire mesh + expansion joints)	Included	—	Included
4	Cleanup and Waste Removal	1 job	$150.00	$150.00

Subtotal: $4,100.00
Sales Tax (8.5%): $348.50
Total Due: $4,448.50

Payment Terms:
Payment due within 15 days of invoice date. Late payments may incur a 2% monthly service charge.
Accepted Payment Methods:
Check, Credit Card, or ACH Transfer
Thank you for choosing A to Z Patios & Decks LLC!
We appreciate your business.

CHAPTER THIRTY-SEVEN

IT DIDN'T TAKE LONG in the morning to find a contractor to drop by and give me a quote. I hired them on the spot. The sooner the patio was done, the better. When it got any colder and the ground froze, it would be a lot harder for them to have it cured properly.

I'd been ignoring Vanessa's texts. She was being too nosy, asking too many questions. And writing an article about people lost to Moon Lake? No thanks, I didn't want to go near that with a ten foot pole. Especially not now—not after what I'd discovered.

She'd been texting multiple times a day—it was almost like she thought we could pick up where we left off as teens. But I wasn't that Grace anymore. I hadn't been for a long time.

It didn't surprise me when she knocked on the door that afternoon. Eventually, I would have to face her.

She was fidgeting on the porch, shifting nervous energy back and forth from one side to the other when I opened the door.

"Oh thank god you're okay, Grace! I've been texting

you and getting no response." She pushed her way past me and walked in my house like she had an open invitation.

"Ummm.. sure—why don't you come in so we can talk?" I didn't even attempt to hide the sarcasm. She turned and looked at me, as though I caught her off guard.

"Why are you being so weird?" She wrinkled her nose and for a second, I *was* fifteen-year-old Grace with her best friend. But, no. It couldn't be. I sighed, my shoulders slumping.

"I feel like you're trying to pick up where we left off, and I would rather… not." I saw hurt written all over her face and I wished I could have picked up the words and stuffed them back in my mouth, but I couldn't. We couldn't be friends and it was best to let her know upfront.

"It's this about the article?" Vanessa said quietly but I heard the edge to her tone… a thread of anger building.

"No, it's not that. But I don't want to participate and I would very much appreciate it if you left my father out of your article. I don't want to drag my past all up again. But I'm not the same Grace I was as a kid. And I don't think it's realistic to try to force a friendship now." I tried to give her an explanation. She deserved closure. Not like last time.

"I can't believe after all this time, we have reconnected. You're right, I *did* think we were picking up where we left off. You were like a sister to me, Grace, and you fucking *ghosted* me!" Her voice reached a high pitch, growing louder.

"I know. I have no excuse. Really. I was young and stupid. I was having a hard time at college. Well, there's no excuse, honestly. I never meant to stop talking to you altogether. But it was over ten years ago. And I was glad we reconnected. And I was hoping to clear the air. But I don't want to rebuild our old friendship." I winced at saying the words out loud. It took everything in me to be so direct. But I didn't want to leave a window of opportunity. I didn't want to give her hope I would change my mind.

"I honestly can't believe this! I fucking can't. I don't even know what to say. I don't. This is... I don't know. I didn't do anything to you!"

"No, you didn't. This isn't about you doing anything wrong! It's me. I can't explain it to you. And I'm so sorry."

"I always felt like you were hiding something. Is that what this is about?" She looked around the living room like she was going to see my secret sitting there, waiting to be revealed. I snorted, despite myself. She was right. Of course she was fucking right, which is why we couldn't be friends. This was my exact fear—that she would figure everything out eventually.

I couldn't take the risk. For me or for her.

She would never know it, but part of it was to protect her. From knowing. From having to make a decision.

"Grace, don't do this again." Her eyes always were the window directly to her soul. I saw the pain so clearly, it made my heart ache. "Whatever it is, we can fix it. You were like my sister. I can't lose you again." A tear ran down her cheek and she swiped it away.

I found it hard to speak. I barely whispered, "I'm so sorry. It's not meant to be." Even I heard the "bullshit" in my voice. It sounded so fake.

Her neck flushed and then her cheeks. What was hurt turned into anger in a flash.

"I won't give you a chance to do this again, you know," she spat at me. "So if this is your decision, it's forever." She said it like we were twelve making a blood pact. I nodded and looked down at my feet.

"That's fair," I said. I didn't want to say anything else to make her feel worse, but I was ready for her to leave. I needed this moment to be over. I needed to sit in the pain of it. If she needed to be angry to feel less hurt, then I wanted that for her too.

"And stay away from my parents too. They don't need you stopping by there either." She practically hissed this at me. I pulled my head back, like she had slapped me. I knew it was deserved but she made it sound like I'd been trying to cozy up to her parents.

I bit my lower lip until it hurt and stepped back as she stormed out of my house, slamming the door behind her. It was for the best.

I wouldn't do to Vanessa what my mother had done to her sister. I couldn't even let her be in that position.

But the loss hit me in the gut as I stared at the closed door, the quiet screaming louder than any sound she could have made. I'd been cold—deliberately so—every word measured, every emotion locked down just long enough to get her out the door. I told myself it was necessary. That if I let myself feel, even for a second, I'd beg her to stay and doom us both.

But now the door was shut, and there was nothing left to hold me upright. I'd done what I needed to do to protect her, and the cost of it finally came due. My legs gave out, my knees slamming into the floor, as if my body had decided to surrender before my mind could. The air felt too thick to breathe.

I realized then that I'd lost her—the last important person in my life—not to death, but to absence. To distance. To a choice I'd made with my hands shaking and my heart already breaking. Another permanent loss, carved into me like all the others.

She didn't have to be dead for me to mourn her. This ending deserved its own kind of grief. And as I folded in on myself, alone on the floor, I understood that some goodbyes don't come with cremations—just an empty room and the unbearable weight of what will never come back.

CHAPTER THIRTY-EIGHT

IT WAS strange how comforting a house could become when you'd finally decided to make it your own. The TV hummed low in the background—the first time I'd turned it on since being back. The blue light washed over the living room, soft and flickering, throwing long shadows across the walls. A detective show was starting to play, the kind that promised twists and dark secrets. The irony wasn't lost on me.

I sat cross-legged on the couch, a bowl of popcorn half-finished, when my phone buzzed with an email confirmation from my boss.

Remote status approved. We'll coordinate in-person work as needed.

I exhaled, the kind of exhale that feels like you've been holding it for years. The decision felt final now. No need to return to the city. This house, my mother's house, was officially mine—and for better or worse, I was staying put.

I leaned back into the couch, letting the old floorboards creak beneath me as if the place was finally settling too. I'd spent the last week fixing leaks, repainting trim, and boxing up pieces of her life that were too painful or too meaningless to keep. For the first time in a long time, I was not in motion. I was just… here.

I smiled to myself, almost giddy as the show's theme music swelled. Maybe this was what peace felt like.

Then the knock came. It was soft at first—almost polite. Just *three gentle taps* against the door.

Vanessa, I thought automatically. Would she come back to plead? Part of me hoped so. It would be impossible. An impossible friendship.

I waited, and another knock sounded—sharper this time. *Harder.* It rattled the frame, a sound that didn't belong in a quiet house.

I frowned. Definitely not Vanessa.

A cold current of unease slid down my back. The TV kept playing, voices muffled behind the glass. I paused it, the silence suddenly too loud, and padded barefoot across the living room.

When I reached the front window, I lifted the curtain an inch—enough to peek through the slit. The sight made my stomach tighten. Thomas' truck. Parked crooked next to my car.

"Goddammit," I whispered. Of all people, of all nights.

I had told him, *clearly*, he was not to come here again. I thought he'd finally gotten the message. Apparently not.

The knock came again, louder. This time he was using his fist. I yanked the door open before he could start again.

"What the hell do you think you're—"

Thomas pushed past me before I could finish, a rush of cold air and heavy boots filling the doorway. His face was flushed, slick with sweat, eyes unfocused but wild. He smelled like dirty socks and cheap whiskey. I've never seen him this disheveled. But his drunk and angry entrance reminded me of my father.

"Don't start with me," he snapped, pacing in the living room. "I've had enough of your righteous crap."

"You can't—" I started, but he cut me off again, voice cracking with a cross between rage and desperation.

"I *told* you to sell, didn't I? You could've made this easy. I *hoped* you'd have more sense than your mother. But no, you had to dig in your heels—like she did." His words made me blink. *What?*

"Thomas," I said slowly, trying to keep my tone steady. "You're drunk. Sit down, and we'll—"

"Don't tell me what to do!" he roared, slamming a hand against the wall. The picture frames rattled. "You think you can sit up here on this damn property and pretend none of it matters? You have no idea what you're sitting on."

"I know enough to know it's *mine,*" I shot back, heat rising in my chest. "And you don't get to threaten me in my own home."

His jaw tightened. For a second I think he might hit me. Then he laughed—a short, ugly bark of laughter that made my skin crawl.

"You're just like her then, aren't you?" he muttered. "Stubborn, self-righteous, acting like you're above it all. Your mother wouldn't listen either. Look where it got her."

My pulse raced. "What the hell is that supposed to mean?"

He stopped pacing, eyes darting toward me, then away. "You don't need to know."

"The men who came up here last week," I pressed, the memory flashing back, "They said you owed them money. They were threatening you."

Thomas's face twitched. "That's got nothing to do with you."

"The hell it doesn't!" I snapped, stepping closer. "You brought whatever this is to my door. Why?"

He didn't answer. He looked at me—a long, simmering stare like it was peeling back my skin. When he finally spoke, his voice was quieter but more dangerous than before.

"You think you know everything about this place, don't you? About your precious family. You don't know half of it."

A coldness gripped my stomach. "What are you talking about?"

He chuckled again, hollow. "You don't know, do you? What your mother did?"

The room tilted slightly, as if the air pressure had changed. "What—"

"She killed him," Thomas said simply. "Your father. I *know.*"

My breath caught. "That's not true."

"Oh, it's true," he sneered. "I saw my father's investigation notes. And when I came and made her an offer no sane person would turn down, she said it wasn't an option. Something was keeping her here. Evidence maybe? Old blood soaked into the floors? What was it?" His eyes scan the room as if a pool of blood would still be sitting here thirteen years later.

The words hit me like a slap. My mind reeled, trying to

process, to find footing on ground that was suddenly crumbling.

"You're full of shit," I managed, but my voice shook, betraying me.

He stepped closer, his shadow stretching long across the floor. "She was stubborn. Just like you. You think you're so different?"

"You were here," I whispered. "Weren't you? You tried to get her to sell by scaring or bullying her too. She had a heart attack, but that was because of you, wasn't it?"

Thomas's eyes flickered. He didn't deny it. Instead, he shrugged. "I made her an offer. She didn't take it."

The realization landed with an almost physical weight.

"She didn't have to make it so hard," he growled. "I told her it'd be easier to let go. But she wouldn't listen. She thought she could fight everyone. Well, maybe she should've learned when to quit."

Something inside me snapped. The fear that had been crawling under my skin hardened into a sharpness.

"You bastard," I hissed. "You pushed her until she broke. She didn't die from a heart attack—she died from *you.*"

Thomas's face twisted. "You don't know what you're talking about."

He grabbed my wrist, squeezing hard enough to make me gasp. "You're going to sign those papers. Tomorrow. You're going to sell this land, and you're going to stop pretending you're a hero."

"Let go of me," I said, but he didn't.

His grip tightened. His other hand lifted, shoving me backward. I stumbled into the coffee table, the popcorn bowl crashing to the floor, kernels scattering like white bugs. My heart pounded against my ribs.

"Thomas!" I shouted, trying to push him away. He was too strong, too close. His breath was hot and sour on my face.

"You don't get it," he spat. "You *can't* win this. I'm not going to stop because you're a grieving daughter. You either give it up or—" He didn't finish.

Because I shoved him then, hard, using all the strength I had. He stumbled back against the fireplace mantel, his arm hitting one of the urns—my father's. The metal one. It wobbled dangerously but didn't fall.

"Get out!" I screamed.

He laughed again, bloodshot eyes wild. "Just like her. Just like her—" He lunged.

We crashed into the side of the couch, the two of us tangled, grunting, breathless. He grabbed at my shoulders, trying to pin me. I twisted, reaching for anything—the lamp, the remote, the edge of the mantel. My fingers brush cold metal.

The urn.

I seized it, barely registering the weight. He was shouting—a name, maybe mine—and then my arm swung.

The sound was thick, sickening. Metal on bone.

Thomas froze mid-motion, eyes wide. For a heartbeat, he looked surprised. Then he collapsed forward, dead weight hitting the floor with a dull, final thud.

I dropped the urn. It rolled once, slow, leaving a faint smear across the rug. For several seconds, I couldn't move. The TV flickered again, forgotten. In the distance, the refrigerator hummed to life, oblivious. I stared down at Thomas's still form, the dark stain beginning to bloom beneath his head.

My breath came in shallow gasps.

I took a step back, nearly tripping over the edge of the couch. My hands were trembling. My mind was a spinning void of shock and denial. I didn't mean—I desperately had wanted him to stop—

The urn sat where it landed, dented slightly, my father's initials glinting in the dim light like an accusation.

The clock on the wall ticked loudly, each second stretching like a lifetime. I could hear my pulse pounding in my ears. Outside, a dog started barking, far away. I thought of the truck still in the driveway.

The room swayed. Lilac filled the room, permeating every pore in my nostrils. The room dimmed suddenly… blackness.

CHAPTER
THIRTY-NINE

I'M UPSTAIRS *in my bedroom, reading a book. It's already pretty late, and my father, drunk as usual, stormed out. Off to the bar, my mom told me. I realize that was hours ago. I shift uncomfortably, hating myself for even being worried. My mother is downstairs, probably cleaning the house or watching late night TV.*

What a great Thanksgiving break it's been. Dad had been drunk more of the time than not. He looks and smells disgusting these days—like it was oozing from every pore.

And what used to be an occasional night at the bar has turned into a nightly occurrence. He would already be drinking at home and get annoyed with my mom and peel off in his truck.

Part of me hoped when I went off to college, things would get better. They hadn't. It was so much worse. I couldn't even look him in the eye anymore. I'd shown up for Thanksgiving and my mom had a black eye. One she couldn't hide. And what looked like a busted lip.

The rev of my father's truck as it lurches to a halt, probably inches from the house, makes my entire body tense. He tromps his way up the front porch steps and bangs in through the front door, slamming it behind him.

I have no idea what he could possibly find to be mad at my mother about now but his voice gets louder, booming through the ceiling, slurred and angry. Spewing insults and accusations one after the other. My mother doesn't argue back but, moments later a squealing sound makes me sit up straight. He's hurting her.

I freeze at the edge of the bed. My skin crawls. The room smells like cedar with a strong metallic scent under it, like the last time he hit the mailbox and tore the paint. A second cry—not the crispness of pain but more raw and small and human.

The hair on the back of my neck prickles and a chill runs down my spine. Another cry, and I'm on my feet. I stand there at my bedroom door, wondering what I should do.

"I'll fucking kill you, Heidi."

"Patrick, please stop. Grace…"

"Shut up! Shut up, shut up, shut up." My father doesn't even sound like himself.

Something snaps. Maybe a lamp, maybe wood—the sound is bright and final. My mother's reply is a half-choke; it tears something loose in me, a cord I didn't know was there. My heartbeat drums in my throat. I am at the top of the stairs and then I am flying down them, each step a drumbeat, the house a tunnel funneling me toward the sound.

They're behind the couch, the living room a landscape of overturned cushions and cheap framed pictures. My mother is staggering slightly, her hair falling in a halo around her face. My father is a shadow over her, hands hard at her throat, his face a mask of drink and fury. He pins her to the wall by the fireplace as if she's nothing more than a thing to wedge into a corner.

Her face drains. The color leaves like the light at dusk. Her fingers claw at his wrists, nails scratching, and his grip tightens; his mouth opens and closes like a fish's, useless with the breath stolen from her. The word he said—kill—hangs in the air and tastes like iron.

My mind explodes. A buzzing in my ears gets so loud—like a bomb went off and I can't hear what's happening anymore. My vision clouds and I barrel into my father.

"Get off of her!" I shriek, not even recognizing my own voice. I lunge toward him.

We collide. The room lurches. For an impossible second I think of nothing but the impact: the thud of bodies, the smell of his cologne turned sour by liquor, the slap of fabric. There's a CRACK—not the nice crack of wood breaking but a harsher sound, as if a bone has been insulted. He goes down almost too easily, like a weighted coat on a chair. I'm on top of him, adrenaline making my fingers white and clumsy.

My mother gasps, a terrible, hopeful sound. She scrabbles free, lungs heaving. Her hand finds her throat, fingers trembling, nails leaving crescent moons of white. She looks past me—past the sweat on my lip, past the bleeding split on my knuckle, to wherever the line between safety and disaster might be.

I turn, bracing for him to lunge at me again—but he doesn't move. My father is sprawled beside the fireplace, his body twisted at an odd angle. For a heartbeat, I can't understand what I'm seeing. Then it hits me. When I tackled him, his head must have struck the brick hearth.

There's a dark smear along the corner of the fireplace. Fresh blood glistens there, catching the light. A thicker pool seeps out beneath his head, spreading slow and steady across the floor.

My breath catches. My chest tightens as if a fist has closed around my lungs. I'm shaking so violently I can hear my teeth clicking. The room tilts, colors washing out until only the red seems real.

The scent of lilac drifts through the air—sharp and familiar, like the sachets my mother used to hide in drawers. Then her arms are around me, warm and trembling, pulling me down before my legs can give out. The lilac suffocates me. My mother's voice fades. And then… nothing.

I came back to the present time, shaken by what was distinctly a memory, not a dream. My breath caught, shallow and erratic, as my eyes locked on the corner of the fireplace. The crack in the brick was still there—thin, jagged, the same as in the memory. It was real. *It was all real.*

I blinked rapidly, but the truth didn't fade with the motion. It solidified instead, heavy and cold in my chest. I knew it was true. It was me all along.

This—this was what my mother wanted to protect me from. Not the world. Not other people. *Myself.*

A tremor ran through my hands. The air felt too thin, the room too bright. My stomach turned over as the memory bled into the present, the two realities twisting together until I couldn't tell which one hurt more.

And then I remembered what I did tonight.

No. What I've done again.

The silence pressed down like a weight. I turned my head, slowly, as if delaying the inevitable would change it. Thomas lay sprawled on the floor, his arm bent unnaturally beneath him. There was a spreading puddle of dark, glistening red beneath his head—thick and steady, the color almost black in the dim light of the TV.

For a moment, I couldn't move. My brain refused to process the shape of him, the stillness. The smell of iron reached me, sharp and nauseating.

Finally, I forced myself forward. My knees hitting the

floor beside him. I reached out—hesitated—and pressed two fingers to his neck. The skin was already cooling.

I didn't need to check his pulse to know. But I did anyway.

And when I felt nothing—nothing but silence—the worst part wasn't that he was dead. It wasn't that I killed him. It was that deep down inside, a part of me wasn't surprised.

CHAPTER FORTY

I PACED, tracing the same worn path across the floor, my thoughts looping back on themselves. What would they see if they looked too closely? What had my mother done in moments like this—when panic clawed at her throat, when instinct told her to run but responsibility forced her to stay? I tried to summon her steadiness, the way she always seemed to know which pieces of herself to hide and which to present.

My chest tightened until each breath felt shallow and borrowed, like the air might run out if I took too much of it. I sank into a chair, fingers tangled in my hair, and for a moment the careful walls I'd built began to splinter. Every option felt wrong, every choice heavy with consequences I couldn't see yet but knew would hurt. I thought of all the ways this could go badly, how one mistake could draw the wrong kind of attention, how quickly concern could turn into suspicion.

The not knowing gnawed at me, hollowing me out, and I pressed my palms to my eyes as if I could block the world out entirely. I had never felt so small, so unprepared, suspended in a moment where doing nothing was dangerous and doing something felt just as terrifying.

Eventually, I turned off the part of my brain that wanted to dissolve into a puddle of tears and heartache. I couldn't panic. I didn't know what to do. I don't know how my mother did what she did. Protected me. Protected the family name. My mind flashed to his truck parked outside. I had to get rid of it first. Even if my driveway was mostly hidden by trees, the less time it sat there, the safer. It was possible Dotty had already seen it. I needed to move it before she came over to check on me.

I knew once I made the decision to move his truck, that was it. There would be no turning back. Heaving in a deep, shaky breath, I stood up, wiping my sweaty palms on my pant legs. I took a step toward the body. Watching every step, I crouched down beside him.

Avoiding looking at his face—or the way his head laid in a puddle of blood, I grappled with his pants pockets, searching for his keys and phone. Palming them, I stood, making sure there was no blood on me.

I opened the coat closet and dug around and found a beanie cap. I tied my hair into a bun and pulled the hat down over it. It wasn't the best disguise, but it would have to do. I grabbed an old coat from the back of the closet, one that might have even been my father's. It was musty, and putting it on gave me the heebie jeebies. I took my own cell phone out of my pants pocket and set it on the coffee table. I stuffed my wallet and house keys in its place.

I slunk out to the truck and turned it on, rolling out of the driveway and down the street. I waited until I was around the corner to turn the headlights on.

I drove more carefully than I'd ever driven in my entire life. At first I had no idea where I was going but then I remembered a mention of a hazardous worksite on the outskirts of town in one of the articles about Thomas' transactions.

I avoided as many residential streets and brightly lit businesses as I could. I sat up tall, but kept the hat pulled down. Anyone who saw me drive by could ascertain I was Thomas if they didn't look too hard. I was just a shadow in the cab of the truck.

As I pulled into the work site I'd read about, I killed the headlights, not wanting any passersby to notice me pulling in. But thankfully, traffic seemed excessively light.

I parked the truck and slid out, taking the keys with me. Slipping into the shadows, I walked at a clipped pace. Soon, I was rounding a corner where I could enter a walkway around Moon Lake. I looked around cautiously and flung the keys. I watched as they sailed through the air and waited for the quiet PLUNK as they hit the water.

Pulling his cell phone out of my pocket, I tossed that next, squinting as it hit the water and sank. I exhaled, steadying myself.

I didn't have a plan for how to get home. It was too far to walk in the cold because I had to lose my hat. And jacket. I was grateful for the thick sweatshirt I was wearing underneath, but it wouldn't do much with the cold biting air. My breath came out in foggy puffs.

I continued down the path until I was about to enter a clearing. I knew in another few hundred feet, I'd be able to see Main Street. There were a lot of businesses there. Glancing along the trail, I saw a trash can next to a bench.

I paused and peeled off the jacket first, tossed it into the trash can. Next, I pulled off the hat and threw it in. I yanked the hair tie out of my hair, letting my waves cascade down around my shoulders. I shook them out, and continued walking along the path.

Right before the clearing opened to Main Street, I scanned the open businesses. The lights at Bleeding Brews were warm and welcoming. I could use a hot coffee. I had a long night ahead of me.

I slipped into the coffee shop and placed my order. I felt like everyone could see inside my mind and knew exactly what I had done. While the barista was making my coffee, I excused myself to use the restroom.

Standing at the sink mirror, I examined my face. Did I look like I'd just killed a man? I was shocked to see I looked the same. I didn't know what I expected, but I thought I'd look at myself and see an obvious marker indicating who I was. What I'd done. A murderer. Killed a man.

Again. I ran my hands under the warm water and dried them slowly before returning to the Order Pick Up counter. I grabbed my cup and slipped back out into the cool air. There would be a few drivers waiting out in front of the bars to give drunk patrons a ride, so I made my way in that direction.

I found an available ride and collapsed into the backseat, pulling my collar up around my face and mumbling an address a few blocks away from mine. When the driver pulled to a stop, I had my cash ready and I passed it over to him and slid out of the car before he could ask me anything else.

I disappeared into the shadows between two houses and shortcut my way back to my own street. I cut through a backyard, keeping close to the treeline and managed to make it to my own front door without setting off any motion sensor lights.

Sliding my keys from my pocket, I unlocked the door and stumbled inside, closing and locking it quickly behind me.

Inside, I leaned against the door, panting while my heart raced. My stomach rolled, threatening to empty its contents as I took in the scene I had left. The strong metallic scent of blood, the popcorn that had scattered the room—bits of it sticking in the puddle of blood. I was pretty sure I would never eat popcorn again.

I sank down to the floor and sipped my drink. I needed to get busy in the backyard, but for a minute, I let myself drink this coffee. Even if it was curdling my stomach, I needed the caffeine. I swiped at a tear and forced myself to put up my steel walls, because this was not the time to break down. It wasn't even an option.

I had a lot of work to do. I could cry myself to sleep when the sun came up.

CHAPTER FORTY-ONE

STUFFING MY FEELINGS DOWN, I pulled myself together. The moon was a thin, fingernail slice above the trees, silvering the frost into a brittle, false calm. Each exhale tasted like my coffee and that hint of metallic clung to me. The backyard was a shadowed outline I used to know by day—the compost heap, the way the neighbor's porch light splashed across the fence. At night it felt like a different place entirely.

The soil swallowed secrets as easily as it did his name. And now the ground took another name. In the shed, I pulled out a shovel. I was pretty sure it was the one from my memory. The shovel my mother bought after I killed my father.

I moved slowly, as if speed would betray me to the light. My fingers were numb in spite of the new jacket I snagged from the coat closet; I used to think cold sharpened you, made you deliberate. Now it bluntly reminded me I was alive.

For a moment, I was ridiculous enough to imagine the yard was lit by moonlight for a ceremony. I didn't think about technique. I didn't count or plan. Those might have been useful things if I were trying to teach someone else how to do what I was doing, but I wasn't; I was only moving through the motions, and the motions were carried by a current of guilt that had no compass. My hands remembered weight; my body remembered how to keep going when the world was a single task. All the manuals in the world don't teach you how to bury a secret of this magnitude.

I was ashamed that a part of my mind calculated the possibilities in small, tidy measures: how long it would be before anyone noticed Thomas was missing, what my alibi would look like if I had to make one up. That calculation was a cold, mechanical thing that sat beside the grief like a second heart.

I closed my eyes and let all the images I couldn't bear to look at roll like a film behind my lids: my father's face, the tilt of the other man's shoulders, the sound of things finally stopping.

I moved through it like a ghost in a place that used to be home, and for the first time since I made whatever decisions put me in this place tonight, I allowed myself to think of possibility—not the legal kind, not a future rewritten like a tidy novel, but the possibility of confession, of collapse, of a descent into consequences more absolute than I could imagine.

Shaking my head, I returned to shoveling. The minutes ticked on. The hours passed. I took breaks, my hands and legs shaking with the effort. But I needed to get it done. The grave was finally big enough. I barely felt able to continue, but I had no choice. I had no sister's life to ruin by calling and asking for help. I had to do this on my own.

I dragged the body to the grave, pushing it in. Then I

began shoveling the dirt in, covering him slowly. I closed my eyes when the dirt started to fall on his face, covering it one scoop at a time. I couldn't bear to watch that happening. As much as I hated Thomas, surely he was important to someone.

Dawn was breaking when I finally got the last dirt moved back in and patted down. I paused and stared at the obvious grave. It couldn't be left this way. Dotty would have questions. And the company coming to pour the patio would find it strange. So I started clearing the grassy parts in a much bigger area. Marking where exactly I wanted the patio poured.

Directly over where I knew my father was buried and over Thomas' body as well. I cleared a big enough area reaching to the back steps. This was where the patio would be. Now it looked like I'd started the process.

I put the shovel back in the shed and headed inside to clean up everything else.

I didn't question why my mother had four bottles of bleach stored in the pantry, but I was thankful for it. Cleaning inside took me several more hours. The urge to light a match and burn the whole house down, me inside, came and went in roller coaster waves as exhaustion took over me.

When I was done, I stood in the shower and let the hot water cascade down on me. I crumbled to the shower floor, crouched on my knees, scrubbing at myself with soap. I couldn't wash the night off me. I probably never would be able to. The stain of what I'd done was as permanent as a birthmark.

At last, I collapsed into bed, hair dripping wet still. I burrowed under the blankets and let the nightmare pound down on me.

• • •

My mother is floating toward me, holding her arms out to me. "It's okay my love. It's okay. You had no choice." Remember what I said…

If you have this note, you don't have me.
Remember, you're the last of the family tree.
If you need me, I can't be there.
None of this was ever fair.
If you need to know what you can't see,
Just remember the family tree.

I sat upright, drenched in sweat, my hands callused, my back and shoulders stiff. Glancing at the clock, I saw it was afternoon. I only slept a couple of hours, but the dream I'd had of my mother reciting the poem I'd found in the urn had woken me up, unable to doze off again.

I dug around in my nightstand where I'd shoved the note. Pulling it out, I read it again. What was she trying to tell me?

Family tree? We didn't have a lot of extended family. Family tree? Was that code for the apple tree? Suddenly it hit me. The picture on the wall downstairs.

I hobbled downstairs, each step painful to every muscle and joint in my body, to the framed photos hanging on the wall. Old school photos of mine, pictures of me in various costumes on Halloween, Christmas morning. And there, the one that didn't belong. It had caught my eye before, curious why my mother had hung it up with these others.

In the photo, my mother was standing underneath her apple tree in the backyard. She was not smiling, and I don't know who could have taken the picture. Lifting the hinges on the back to take the photo out, I pulled it out and flipped it over. And there in my mother's loopy handwriting was a letter. To me.

I stared at the letter for the longest time. I should have felt something. But it was like I felt everything and nothing all at once, and I was numb. I slipped the photo back into the frame and put it right back on the wall. I suddenly felt very dizzy.

All my emotions swirling, the stress poured down on me. The room swayed and the scent of lilacs wafted by me.

I feel the room slipping away and then… blackness.

To my sweetest Grace,
If you've found this, you probably know the truth. And I'm probably no longer of this earth. I knew this day would come- no matter how long I tried to prolong it. It was inevitable.

What happened that night- you weren't to blame. I know you. And I know you'll be thinking you must be a terrible person. What kind of person would do such a thing? But you didn't have a choice. You saved my life.

I'm so sorry I couldn't let you come home, but it was the only way I knew to protect you. When you woke up the next morning and I realized you'd forgotten everything- or blocked it out, I couldn't risk you being here and possibly remembering. I needed you to be far away, and safe from the memories this house held.

But if you're reading this, I know you must be back, and you must have remembered everything.

Please- don't let this ruin the rest of your years. Don't let this deprive you of the life you want to live. A happy life. That's all I ever wanted for you. I'm so sorry I failed to protect you when you were a child. I'm so sorry I put you in a position where you had to do what you did, just so we could see to live another day.

Please, if you can do one thing- live your life as the brightest star I've always known you to me.

Love,
Mom

EPILOGUE

I POUR myself a steaming cup of coffee, adding milk and sugar. Holding my mug in one hand, I open the back door and step out onto my new patio. It's only been a week since it was cured but I've already had a small table and chairs set delivered.

Even though the air has a damp chill to it of late fall, I make my way out and sit in the chair. The coldness bites through my thick sweatpants.

Wrapping my hands around the mug, I let the steam warm my face. My life in the city feels as far away, as long ago, as high school. My neighbor, Dotty, pokes her head over her fence.

"Cold morning to be outside, Grace. But that was smart having your patio poured now. You'll be glad you did it before winter when spring comes and you can enjoy it right away." She nodded and smiled. What was she doing outside? She'd probably seen me from the window and bundled herself up to come out and talk to me.

"The cold doesn't bother me. But you're right. Spring will be so beautiful out here. We'll have to have a little brunch out here one day," I offer. She's not able to hide the glee from her voice, like an overexcited kid, when she responds.

"Yes, I would love that! That's how neighbors should be! Oh Grace, I'm so glad you've moved back." I smile and she mumbles about being too cold and goes back to her own house, making happy little noises all the way in.

My phone rings and I pull it free from my pocket to answer. It's the attorney who handled the estate. He's going over a few things, but I wasn't paying attention.

"Ms. Jenkins? Are you still there?"

"Oh yes, sorry. What was that again?"

"I said, I have a realtor I could refer you to, if you're ready to put the house up for sale." He repeated himself.

"Oh, no thank you. That won't be necessary. I've decided to stay." He seems surprised and asks what made me change my mind.

"Oh, I don't know, I guess I realized how much it felt like home." I shrug even though he can't see me. We finish the call and I hang up.

I don't know why I'm still here—I can't put my finger on why I feel compelled to say. It's like something drawing me. I know there's a reason, but it's on the edges of my mind. I couldn't pin it down.

I'm going to make Bleeding Hearts Valley my home again. The people are different here than in the city. I can be a regular at the coffee shop and the library and be friendly with those folks without them asking me to go out for drinks all the time, like the people I met in the city.

As long as that pushy realtor, Thomas, doesn't come by again, trying to bully me into selling, everything's going to be great.

ALSO BY SARA LEA

Also by Sara Lea:

Love & Lies Series of Domestic Thrillers:

- The Art of Disappearing (Prequel)
- The Art of Dishonesty
- The Art of Desperation
- The Art of Deception

Standalone Thrillers:

Home Sweet Home

The Game Night

Shared World Standalone Thrillers:

Family Tree, part of The Bleeding Hearts Valley Thrillers

Thriller/Horror Stories/Novellas:

Final Order, part of the Fight Like a Final Girl Collection

Santa Baby, part of the Holiday Horrors Collection

The Neighbors Secret

The Last Ten Minutes, micro-fiction (ten minute read)

Speed Date, part of the Love You To Death Collection

Bad Bunny, Part 1 of On the Hunt Duology

Jack Rabbit, Part 2 of On the Hunt Duology

Quiet Ones, part of the Deadly Silence Collection

Follow on Amazon, Facebook (Sara Lea, Author), and Instagram (@saraleabooks) for updates!

www.ingramcontent.com/pod-product-compliance
Lightning Source LLC
La Vergne TN
LVHW091115080826
845145LV00008B/1925

9781953476210